Operation Pandora

Leon Michaels

Books by Leon Michaels

The Path Home

From the Mists of Darkness

Task Force Nemesis

Tales From The Bench

The Hanover Throne

The Echelon Factor

The Morbius Expedition

The Bellus Project

Three Against The Darkness

Random Acts Of Science Fiction

Willem

Today is Yesterday's Tomorrow

"The Crane Equation Trilogy"

The Crane Equation: The Early Years

The Crane Equation: Rebuilding a Nation

The Crane Equation: The Crane Legacy

"The Black Ops Series"

Operation Damocles

Operation Dokkaebi

Operation Yofune-Nushi

Operation Kartikeya

The Black Orchid

The Twenty-First Special Operations Group: Book One: Family

The Twenty-First Special Operations Group: Book Two: Operators

Operation Heracles

Acknowledgements

To all of the helicopters pilots that have flown into harm's way to carry us Infantry types out of harm's way, and into the waiting hands of Doctors, Nurses, Corpsmen/Medics.

Thanks, does not seem enough.

As always, to my loving Bride.

This is a work of Fiction. Any similarities to individuals past or present is unintentional and purely a coincidence. Any similarities to any individual in the future is pure Karma.

Whatever it Takes.

Everyone at the headquarters of the Twenty-First Special Operations Group (SOG) were watching a blow by blow attempt by Marine Aviation to extract their Ops Team, call sign Razor on the large monitors along the walls of the headquarters via a drone high overhead.

In the Conference Room, General Sandra Grainger and Lieutenant Colonel Gloria Garcia also had an audio link directly to Team Razor. The two, large wall mounted monitors were further linked to the gun cameras of the Marine Cheyenne Attack Helicopters trying to support Team Razor.

Team Razor had fulfilled their mission of removing a command group of an offshoot FARC organization from Columbia operating in Northern Ecuador. But the weather in the mountains just west of Otavalo Ecuador had prevented extraction, requiring Team Razor to move towards the coast.

Everything began to fall apart as their trail was picked up by the militia group they had hit, and were being closely pursued. The militia was better organized than intelligence estimated, and Razor had to fight their way out of the mountains onto the plains where the weather was reported clear enough for air support.

Razor was ten kilometers from the Pacific Ocean with two men of the six-man team wounded and being boxed in. They were exposed and calling for help.

A Marine Super-Blackhawk flew off the USS Kearsarge II with a four-bird escort of Cheyenne's. As the Cheyenne's made a pass over the militia forces with rockets and guns, the Blackhawk attempted to land and extract Razor. Suddenly the Blackhawk began to fly radically, then climbed as they turned towards the ocean and the Kearsarge. The audio told what had happened.

Both pilots were wounded along with the Starboard door gunner. It would be later known that the Crew Chief, pulled the pilot from his seat, while the wounded Co-Pilot fought to maintain control of the aircraft. The Crew Chief did a quick first aid on the pilot and the door gunner, then crawled into the pilot's seat and took over the aircraft controls. He advised the Kearsarge that he was returning at best possible speed. As with many Marine Crew Chiefs, they had learned how to pilot the aircrafts they were responsible for just in case this very situation happened.

The Kearsarge advise another Blackhawk was being readied along with another flight of Cheyenne's.

High above the battle, Whiskey Nine, one of the Cheyenne's was watching and waiting their turn at strafing the militia. The pilot looked at their available fuel to bingo, having to return to the Kearsarge, then the time it would take for a new group to arrive. The pilot estimated there would be at least a five-minute gap between the two and that was more than enough time for the militia to overrun the people they were trying to protect. The pilot made a decision which nearly everyone listening considered suicide.

"Razor Six, this is Whiskey Niner, do you copy over?"

The voice in Razor Six's ear sounded metallic and without any sense of what sex might be calling him. For all he knew, it was a robot flying the Cheyenne that was calling him.

"Yeah Whiskey Niner, this is Razor Six, over."

The sounds of gunfire were almost deafening over the speakers in the Conference Room.

"Razor, do you have the ability to construct a SPIE line, I say again, can you construct a SPIE extraction line, over?"

"Whiskey, affirmative but it will be short, over."

"Razor, get rigged up, I say again, rig up. When ready I'll come down and you can tie off on my Port wheel strut. Do you copy? Over."

"Whiskey, I copy rig SPIE line and secure to your Port wheel strut. Is that correct, over?"

"Affirmative Razor, and be quick, we are getting near Bingo fuel, Over."

"Roger, working on it now. Over"

"Razor, when ready let me know, I have visual on your location, but not you. Wave once ready so I'll know where to come it at. Over"

"Roger Whiskey Niner, over"

For those watching via the drone link, seconds seemed like minutes, minutes like hours. Tracers could be seen crossing the plain from Razor to the militia and from the militia to the Razor's position. Gun camera footage was showing the Cheyenne's chewing up militia positions and there were bodies lying all around the perimeter encapsulating Razor.

"Whiskey Niner, come and get us out of this shithole, over."

"All Whiskey Elements, cover me, I'm going in."

"Razor, this is Whiskey, here I come, get ready, I'm coming in hot, over."

The Cheyenne Attack Helicopter was the most maneuverable helicopter ever built, but those watching via the drone wondered if they could make a hard stop as they watched the aircraft dive down to Razor. During the dive, the pilot extended their landing gear and locked it into place as the Gunner/Observer was firing as best they could on targets from the extreme angle they were traversing towards the ground.

It seemed as if the Cheyenne was going to nose into the ground when the pilot suddenly flipped the nose up, and added power to maintain lift, then drifted down towards the ground. Razor Six was nearly under the Port wheel when downward motion ceased, and he reached up, wrapped the doubled rope twice around the strut, and hooked it back together with a lockable carabiner to secure it.

"Whiskey, Go, Go, Go! We're tied on, over!"

As Whiskey Nine was lifting, the other three Cheyenne's began their final gun runs, trying to keep the militia's heads down as Whiskey Nine was trying to gain attitude. Whiskey Nine's gunner was basically unloading its remaining ordinance into any target he could find to help lighten the load on the aircraft.

At three hundred feet above sea level, Whiskey Nine went to full emergency power and headed for the ocean.

"Whiskey Flight, this is Haven. We have a convoy coming from Rioverde, suspect local military coming to investigate the noise. Get feet wet ASAP, over."

"Haven, this is Whiskey Five, understand. Wet feet in approximately three, I say again three minutes."

Haven was the call sign the Kearsarge was using for this mission in case their communications were compromised.

The drone followed the Cheyenne's out of the country as they took a diamond formation with Whiskey Nine in the lead with the cargo of men hanging below the aircraft. Once over the water, the flight dropped down as low as possible without dragging the men in the water in order to stay below radar if possible.

"Whiskey Nine, this is Haven. Be advised your landing position is just aft of the island. Medical personal are waiting for your cargo, over."

"Roger Haven. Status of Extraction one, over?"

"Whisky, they are on the deck and have been taken below. Watch for your landing officer as you approach, over."

"Understand Haven, be advised I can see your lights, over."

"Roger Whiskey, Whiskey flight, turn on your running lights, over."

From the Kearsarge's island, four sets of red and white lights suddenly came on off the port side, slightly aft of the ship.

"Whiskey Flight, we have your lights. Bring it home, Over."

Gloria sat at the computer in the Conference Room and punched in a set of numbers which linked the Flight Deck Cameras to her monitors as the Gunner's aboard the Cheyenne's placed their chain guns into a neutral position and safed them, which also turned off their gun cameras.

"Haven, this is Whiskey Nine. Have someone with a sharp knife handy to cut the ropes so I can shift and sit down, over."

"Whiskey Nine, already done, over."

The flight deck cameras showed three helicopter's gaining altitude, then move off to the left of the screen, away from Whiskey Nine which gained attitude, but was coming directly towards the ship. The cameras showed one of the deck crew move out away from the ships island with a pair of flashlight wands and positioned themselves to act as a guide post for Whiskey Nine.

"Pull up Nine, you're too low." Came a disconnected voice over the radio.

Whiskey Nine immediately lifted higher as they approached the ship and began to slow down forward momentum. Soon they were over the flight deck, and went into a hover as men ran out from the island to help control, and stop the swinging motion of the men hanging below the aircraft.

9

The deck officer motioned for Whiskey Nine to begin decent and lower the men to the flight deck. All the time this was happening, the ship was still moving forward and Whiskey Nine had to side slip to stay in position. As soon as the last man, the one nearest the aircraft was in the control of deck personal, one of them cut the rope, releasing Whiskey Nine from its burden.

"Whiskey Nine, you are clear to land, Over."

"Thank you Haven."

Whiskey Nine was guided over to a clear spot and landed under the guidance of the deck officer, then began shut down procedures while the men they had rescued were being taken below for medical treatment. Except for one who although wounded, hobbled over to the aircraft. He stood, being supported by a Corpsman who was trying to get him to go below decks to Sickbay.

Razor Six looked at the aircraft that had just saved his life and the lives of his team. There were bullet holes in various places and the windscreen canopy showed to have taken hits, but none that penetrated into the flight crew.

The canopy lifted and shifted out of the way as first the Gunner rose up out of the cockpit. Razor Six hobbled closer and extended his hand to the Gunner.

"Thanks, is not enough, but still, thanks for saving my ass."

"Hey, I was just along for the ride, Butch made the call to go down and get you. You Razor Six?"

Razor saw the Lieutenant bars on the Gunner's flight suit.

"Maybe so Lieutenant, but if you were my type, I'd give you one hell of a kiss."

"Don't tell Butch that. You just might get kissed."

"Butch the pilot?"

"Yeah, by the way, who are you?"

"Major Patrick Taylor." He looked at the name tag on the flight suit. "Lieutenant Randall."

"Hey Butch, unass that cockpit and meet Major Taylor!" Randall yelled towards the aircraft.

Taylor noticed the pilot appeared to be writing on the knee notebooks all pilots wore. The pilot just waved, then held up a single finger advising them it'd be a minute. The Corpsman was still trying to get Taylor to go below, but even wounded, the Corpsman was no match for Taylor's strength.

The pilot rose up out of the cockpit, hopped down to the flight deck and stood looking at Taylor. Their face was covered by a hideous mask which in the light of the flight deck looked like a deformed witch's face. The mask was to protect the wearer's face from flash fire in the cockpit. They reached up and unfastened the mask, then removed the flight helmet, exposing almost shoulder length red hair. The face beneath the hair was heart shaped, and the smile on the full lips was honest.

"Major Taylor, meet Butch, also known as Captain Karla Welch. Butch be careful, Major Taylor has already stated his intent to kiss us for saving his life."

Butch pulled her flight gloves off and offered her hand to Taylor.

"Pleasure to meet you Major Taylor. Now why don't you let that poor Corpsman take you down and get fixed up before you bleed to death on our flight deck."

Taylor took her hand and just held it.

"Captain Welch, my team owes you a debt I doubt we'll ever be able to pay. Thank you."

11

"No thanks needed Major, we Marines have to stick together."

"Yes, that we do.   Thanks again, Captain Welch. Corpsman, lead the way."

He stopped just short of the hatch leading into the carrier's island and down to Sickbay.   Taylor keyed his radio knowing it was linked to a satellite, directing his call to the Twenty-First SOG.

"Bunker, this is Razor Six, do you copy, over?"

Sandra walked over to the desk phone, punched in four numbers which linked the phone to radio communications.

"Razor Six, this is Actual, go ahead over."

"Whiskey Nine is also Captain Karla Welch.   Can we insure she does not get burned for hazarding her craft to get us out, over?"

"We'll do what we can.   Now go below and see the docs. Actual out."

Sandra broke the connection as Gloria cleared the monitors and shut down the links to the Razor team.

"Gloria, I know we had the weather factored into this operation, but we need to find out how the intelligence on the FARC Militia was bad.   I'm not blaming you, because we both think close to the same, but I would not have approved that mission as planned if our intelligence had those other units nailed down."

"I agree Sandra, but I'm going to wait until tomorrow before I set a few fires.   Pat did one hell of a job getting his people into position to be extracted.   The other side screwed that up big time.   Whiskey Nine had guts to go in like that and lift them out."

"Yeah she did. Well, shut it down, and I'll see you in the morning."

Twelve hours later the Razor Team rode an elevator to the flight deck along with the Blackhawk crew to load onto an Osprey for a trip over to the carrier, the USS Gerald Ford so they could catch a flight in a COD (Carrier On-Board Delivery aircraft) for a trip to the Naval Hospital on Coronado Island.

Taylor had requested that Captain Welch be present when they boarded the helicopter's so each of the team could thank her. He was the last person to board the helicopter, and the last to once again thank her for their rescue. Taylor handed her a card with his name and cell phone number hand written on it.

"Captain, when you folks get back to El Torro, give me a call. I'm buying you and Lieutenant Randall the biggest steak there is."

"Sure, thing Major."

He leaned over close to her, so he could speak without everyone hearing.

"If you get into any trouble about risking your bird coming to get us, call me immediately. I do have a few friends in high places."

"Thank you Major, I just might do that. Now get off my flight deck."

Taylor laughed as he boarded the Osprey. When he looked back at her, she was putting his card in her flight suit breast pocket. He thought to himself that if he didn't already have a female who he was considering marrying, this Captain Welch might be interesting to know better.

What Taylor was not aware of was that Captain Welch had already been grounded, and informed a Board of Inquiry was being formed at the Marine Corps Air Station, El Torro, to determine if the risk she took with her forty-million-dollar aircraft was an acceptable risk.

At the same Taylor, and the wounded were being flown to El Torro, the Wing Maintenance Officer, along with a survey team were flying to the Gerald Ford to inspect her Cheyenne.

The Board

Six days after the extraction of the Razor Team, Karla Welch sat before a five-officer review board to determine if her conduct, the risking of her aircraft during the extraction of a Special Operations Team was justified.

The aircraft had been surveyed to determine extent of damage suffered during the extraction, and the cost of repairing that damage. Staff Sergeant Greg Zeminski, her crew chief had complained that the Survey Team restricted his access to the aircraft during their inspection and from what he could tell from a distance were writing up damage that had nothing to do with the extraction. Damage that did no effect the flight ability of the aircraft or safety of the flight crew.

Karla had made both verbal and written statements before the Board as she now endured sitting and listening to the other pilots of that flight give their versions of what they saw and heard during that mission. They had just sworn in First Lieutenant Morrison, pilot of Whiskey Three, when General Zegers, the Commanding General of the Third Marine Air Craft Wing, entered the room.

The General's entrance stopped the process since he was the reviewing officer in this case, and was prohibited by regulation from being involved, even in the room as an observer while the Board sat. He walked past the desk where Welch and her legal counsel sat, and went directly to the Board's President and laid a thin, manila folder on the desk in front of him. He then turned to Welch and spoke.

"Captain Welch, these proceedings are closed. You are dismissed and can return to duties."

Karla stood and responded.

"Aye-aye Sir."

She gathered up her things and left the room without further comment from anyone in the room. Outside the room she was slightly shaking as she walked down the hall wondering what had just happened. As she turned a corner to go to the buildings exit, she saw her Squadron Commander, Lieutenant Colonel Kilbourne, standing by the doors.

As she approached him, Kilbourne made a slight gesture telling her to be quiet as he opened the door for her. He followed her out the door and about halfway down the sidewalk, he told her to wait until they were at her car before asking any questions.

Karla put her things in her passenger seat, then turned to address her commander.

"Colonel Kilbourne, what the hell just happened?"

"An hour ago, Colonel Sheehan and myself was instructed to report to General Zegers office. We were ushered right in and told to stand out of the way and be quiet. Zegers wasn't alone. There was a one star sitting real relaxed like in a chair. Once we were off to the side, the visitor spoke, saying he would complete his mission at that time."

Kilbourne paused for a second as if to insure he had his facts straight.

"I knew that General, and he certainly isn't aviation. His name is Grainger, and the last time I saw him was at Lejeune. He's a Raider and somewhat of a legend in that outfit. Anyway, he told Zegers that his command would cover any and all repairs to your bird up to two million dollars considering the appraisal is at one point six-three million. He then pulled a document from his briefcase and told Zegers that was the approval of transfer to Third MAW, the maintenance funds once work was complete, and that someone would stop by and pick up the final cost reports on repairing your bird."

"Colonel Kilbourne, I've never heard of such a thing."

16

'Neither have I Butch, but Zegers did not look happy either. But it got real nasty then. General Grainger told him that his people would be very unhappy if you were punished for your actions in saving his people. He then handed Zegers a thin folder which Zegers read. I thought Zegers was going to have a stroke as he read whatever was in that folder. Grainger waited until Zegers closed the folder, then asked him if they had an understanding. Zegers told Grainger he would deal with it."

"What was in the folder?"

"I have no idea Butch, but whatever it was really got Zegers upset. Then it got weird. Grainger got up and handed me the briefcase, then told me that he was certain no formal ceremony would take place all things considered, but to insure you have the contents of the briefcase. Then he left and that was that."

"What's in the briefcase Colonel?"

"Captain Welch, when we return to the Squadron, there will be a small ceremony in which I will award you the Distinguish Flying Cross, then the Navy Cross for your actions in rescuing a Special Operations Team during a classified operation. The actual citations are sealed. Lieutenant Randall will receive the DFC and a Silver Star."

"A Navy Cross for what I did? Who submitted me for such a medal Sir?"

"I have no idea, but the signatures on the paperwork are the Secretary of Defense and Navy, so someone with a lot of stroke made the request. Butch, there is one other thing. Zegers made a call, two actually, after Grainger left. The first was to the Commandant himself. We only heard one side of the conversation, but Zegers wanted to know Grainger's position, assignment, and as I gathered from what I heard, he was told to mind his own business and handle the situation which Grainger presented to him. The next call was to Officer Assignments telling them he wanted you out of his command as quick as possible."

"This is insane Colonel. What did I do wrong?"

"As far as I'm concerned, nothing. Granted, you did nothing more than what that Blackhawk would have done if the crew had not been shot up, but we both know there are still people in this world that do not feel it is right to have a female at the controls of a weapons platform like the Cheyenne. I'm sorry Butch, but let's go get the ceremony over with, some pictures taken for your family, then we just have to wait for those higher than us to make a decision. Also, Zegers said you were still grounded."

Kilbourne then turned and walked to his car, leaving Karla with a dozen unanswered questions. She got into her car and found she had trouble putting the key into the ignition as her hand was shaking. She was upset about what was happening to her and her career, but she did not know what she could do about it at this time.

The ceremony was held in Kilbourne's office with only a photographer in attendance. Later, Lieutenant Randall's was more formal with the Group Commander presenting his medals.

Twenty-four hours later, Karla had her orders. She was going to Headquarters Marine Corps (HQMC) to an unspecified assignment.

The Offer

Karla slowly rolled out of bed so as not to disturb her bed partner as she got up to get ready for work. This was her third playmate in the eight months she had reported to HQMC, and she was already tiring of this one.

Ronald Bogart was the Executive Director of a charity based in Washington, and they had met at a charity function that she had been basically ordered to attend by her boss. They dated for nearly a month before she allowed him in her bed. Lately he had been wanting her to wear her uniform at parties and other functions she attended on his arm, but she refused to allow the uniform to be used in such a way.

She insisted that any nights they spent together would be in her apartment since she had to be at work long before he did and this way she did not have to rush home, change then go to work. She got dressed, then woke him up and left for work without kissing him goodbye.

Karla Welch had a degree in Aerospace Engineering, but since reporting for duty at HQMC, she had been moving paper across her desk in what she considered a meaningless job. She had learned that the last person to occupy her desk was a Corporal. Karla felt she knew what was happening, but with two years left on her enlistment, she was not about to resign her commission regardless of how she was being treated.

Every attempt she made to get fight time, so she could maintain her flight pay was met with one road block after another. It came down to no squadron would allow her near their aircraft. She had become a leper even though everyone treated her with respect.

She was just finishing up her day when a familiar face appeared before her desk. Lieutenant Colonel Michael Conley had been her instructor pilot when she transitioned to the Cheyenne.

Karla had heard she had been promoted, and was in line for a command. She stood in his presence.

"Hey Butch, how you doing?" He offered her his hand.

"Oh, I'm just peachy Colonel. And congratulations on the promotion. Sir."

"Captain, they have given me HMA-467 (Marine Attack Helicopter Squadron 467)."

"That's good to hear Sir."

"Thank you, but there is no place for you there. Now before you get upset, listen to me carefully. I'd fly with you any day, anywhere, but the powers to be will not allow it. I could go to the Commandant and most likely get you assigned, but there are still too many senior officers that still have problems with females in the cockpit of gunships. You were one of the best students I ever taught, and it pains me they have treated you the way you are being treated."

He stood and watched as she began to have tremors in her body. He knew she was angry and holding it back the best she could.

"Karla, get a grip on your emotions because they will do you more harm than good. Now pay close attention to what I am about to tell you. Soon you will be made an offer you certainly can chose not to accept, but accept it. It might not seem all that great a deal for the most part, but I can promise you that you will not regret it."

"What kind of offer Sir?"

"Sorry Butch, that's all I can say at the moment."

"Alright Colonel, and thanks for stopping by."

"Butch, I really wish I could do more, but the politics of this are against it."

Karla offered her hand and they shook hands before he left her cubicle.

She thought about what Colonel Conley had said about accepting the offer she would be made, yet not what the offer might be. Karla knew a lot about Conley, in that both of his parents ended up as General's, and his mother had commanded the forces that put down the California Insurrection with very little destruction or deaths.

Michael Conley was no one's errand boy, so whomever he was fronting for had to have some serious pull. This was a Thursday night, and Ron had a charity auction/ball scheduled tonight meaning she had to get home, and get cleaned up. He had arranged for her to wear a very seductive gown tonight which offered a lot, but gave nothing away. It went well with her dark, red hair and creamy complexion.

As with most of these engagements, Ron used her as eye candy as they moved about the ball room, meeting and greeting the guests and donors to the projects Ron's organization supported. He had once tried to introduce her by her Marine rank and she quietly whispered in his ear if he tried that again, she would cut his cock off and feed it to him. He took her at her word.

Tonight, she was standing next to him smiling as he was talking to an elderly couple whose wife was wearing diamonds which would probably pay for a Blackhawk, when she was startled by being addressed from behind.

"Captain Welch, I would have thought you'd be in your blues tonight."

She turned around to see the Commandant of the Marine Corps and his wife standing behind her.

"Sir, this is not a formal Marine function, sir."

"True, but here I am dressed in my finest. Are you aware that one of the charities Mister Bogart is supporting with this auction is the Soldiers and Sailors homes?"

"No Sir, I was not. I suppose that would be a valid reason to wear my blues Sir."

"Yes Captain, it would. Now at the risk of having my wife smack me up side of the head. May I say you look lovely tonight. Mister Bogart is a lucky man to have you on his arm."

Karla looked at the Commandant's wife who seemed to have an honest smile on her face.

"Thank you, sir."

They moved on as Ron was gently tugging on her arm.

"What Ron?"

"Why didn't you introduce me to the Commandant?"

"He knew your name, so I figured he knew you. And to be honest, that is the first time I have met the Commandant. Now I'm thirsty, let's find a waiter."

The rest of the evening was spent just moving about until the auction. This caused her to be separated from Ron as he did his Master of Ceremonies part, leaving her to fend for herself, or fend off prospective suitors. She was propositioned by two Congressmen, a lobbyist, and the wife of a Senator who hinted that she did not wish to share her with her husband.

When they arrived at her apartment late that night, Ron took two large bags from the trunk of his Mercedes. She asked him what that was for and he said he thought he'd just bring a few things to keep at her apartment, so he did not always have to rush back to his condo to get ready for the day.

"So, you decided to basically move in with me?"

"Well Karla, you won't move in with me, so I thought this would be better."

"No, it's not better. And no, we are not going to live together. I'll drop the gown off at your offices tomorrow."

"What the hell is wrong with you Karla?"

"You made a decision concerning my life without talking to me. I have to put up with such things as a serving Marine, but not from a civilian who is getting more from this relationship than they are giving back. I'm not a high-class whore to hang on your arm at these functions to impress your donors. Good night Ron, and as I said, I'll drop the gown off tomorrow."

Karla left him standing in the parking lot, went into her apartment and carefully removed the gown and laid it out. She took the gown by his offices during lunch the next day because she knew he'd be out for some luncheon and not in his offices.

She spent the weekend cleaning her apartment and reading. Ron never called her which told her he had already moved on, and probably had another female in the wings waiting her turn.

On Tuesday, it was nearing three in the afternoon when the phone of Karla's desk decided to bother her. She answered it as per protocol and received a surprise.

"Captain Welch speaking."

"Whiskey Niner, this is Razor Six, over."

"Who is this?"

"Butch, I once told you to call me if you got into trouble about lifting me and my men out of a crapper. But you didn't call."

She looked at the phones handset as if it had turned into a snake.

23

"I'm sorry, but I do not remember your name sir."

"Taylor, Patrick Taylor, and I'm calling because I promised to buy you the largest steak in town."

"Major Taylor, yes, I remember now. How are you Sir?"

"All healed up. Listen unless you have plans, could you meet me at the Army/Navy Club at six for dinner? No strings, just dinner as I promised."

Karla laughed.

"No problem Major, and I'm glad you chose the Army/Navy Club since there would be no way I could go home and change, then meet that time frame. I'll be there at six. See you then."

Karla cleared her desk just before five and as she was driving to the Club, she tried to remember what Taylor looked like. In the dark on the flight deck, he was dirty, and his face covered with camouflage paint. When he left the ship, he was still partially covered with the paint, so hopefully he would remember what she looked like.

She knew how she looked in uniform, especially since she had hers tailored right to the edge of regulations, plus her rows of ribbons she was required to wear drew a lot of attention. Karla had never been to the Army/Navy Club since it was usually a place Company Grade Officers like herself tended to avoid due to the over whelming amount of Field Grade and Flag Officers that haunted the place.

Karla signed in at the door, notating her assignment at HQMC and she was a guest of a Major P. Taylor. The lobby was busy with officers holding drinks talking to each other and she scanned it for a Marine Major who looked like he was waiting for someone. It caught her by surprise when an Air Force Major in his dress uniform called out to her.

"Captain Welch. Over here."

She took him all in as he came over to her. His rows of ribbons were impressive as was his sets of wings. He was a pilot, and wore jump wings plus a Combat Diver's Badge. He was also about six inches taller than her five feet, four inches, and not unattractive. The Air Force uniform hid any aspect of his build.

"Major Taylor?"

He held his hand out.

"Guilty as charged, Captain."

"Sorry Sir, I thought you was a Marine."

He laughed lightly.

"Captain, two of my men are Marines. In SOCOM, teams tend to be a mixture. Please come with me, we have a table waiting."

"We Major? Is your team here with you?"

"No Captain, just some people I think you'll like meeting. Come on, we also have a waiter standing by to take your order since he has already taken ours."

He guided her through the main dining room to an alcove where a table was set with a man and woman sitting in civilian clothing. Taylor brought her up to the table. The man stood and offered his hand to Karla.

"Captain Welch, it is an honor to meet you. My name is Max and my wife's name is Sandra. Please take a seat and we'll wait until you have selected your choice before we open any discussions with you."

Karla smiled as she analyzed this gentleman. His build was like a bulldog and he was taller than Taylor. His hands were not soft, but calloused from hours of hard work. His face showed the

25

tanning of long hours outdoors, and his hair was cut high and tight, Marine Corps style.

She looked at his wife and thought she was a very attractive woman who did not wear much if any makeup, and she was also tanned from the outdoors. Her short, blond hair was also cut military style and the exposed portion of her biceps in the sleeves of her dress showed form. This woman was an athlete.

Taylor was a gentleman and assisted with her chair, then took the empty chair next to her. She picked up the menu and scanned it. As she was looking at the menu, the waiter moved beside her to take her order. Karla looked up at the waiter.

"Waiter, what do you suggest this evening?"

"Captain, we received a fresh supply of Salmon today, and I must say it looks very nice."

"Fine, I'll have the Salmon."

She then looked at the menu and ordered the vegetables to go with the Salmon and unsweetened Iced Tea. Once the waiter left to place the orders, Max opened the discussion.

"How do you like your assignment at Eight and I?"

"It's alright Sir. I would like to be more productive though."

"Bullshit." This comment came from Sandra. "Captain Welch, you hate your assignment, you hate that you cannot get back into a cockpit, and you just kicked your boyfriend to the curb. Basically, your life sucks. Tell me I'm lying?"

"Ma'am, I don't know who you are, especially to make those comments to me. Major Taylor, thank you for your invitation, but I think I had best leave."

"Keep your ass in that seat Captain, at least until I make my offer to you." Sandra ordered.

26

"Pardon me Ma'am, but who are you to order me to do anything?"

Sandra reached under a napkin on the table and tossed a leather ID folder over to Karla. Karla opened it and was shocked by what she saw inside. She just laid the folder on the table and took a neutral position at the table.

"Does that answer your question Captain?"

"Yes, Ma'am it does." She looked Max. "Colonel Kilbourne said there was a General Grainger, a man, who delivered me from the Board of Inquiry, along with the medals I wear. Was that you sir?"

"Yes, Captain it was. But one thing has bugged me for some time. How did you get the call sign Butch?"

Karla laughed out loud and had to ease her laughing before answering.

"General, while in flight school, every peckerwood in the course, and some of the support personal hit on me for the first month. It got to the point that the male of the species thought I was gay, a lesbian, since I refused them, and one of the students started calling me Butch and it stuck. I'm not gay, but I did sleep with a girl while in college just to see what the big deal was all about. I was not impressed. But that call sign has also kept a few men from making moves on me, but the flip side is a few more women than I'd like has also hit on me. Does that answer your question sir?"

Max chuckled. "Yes, it does, thank you."

"Now General. Damn, this can get confusing."

"Captain, for the ease of communication, just refer to us as Max and Sandra. Neither of us will consider it disrespectful on your part."

"Thank you, Max. What I was going to ask was, what did you give General Zegers that caused him to cancel the Board of Inquiry?"

Max never answered as Sandra spoke.

"Pat."

Major Taylor never commented, but stood up and went to the entrance of the alcove and took up a position, so no one could enter. Karla looked at what Taylor was doing, then back at Sandra.

"Captain Welch, Karla, I'm not sure you know, but my job was with Intelligence. What I am about to tell you is highly classified and I do not have a Non-Disclosure Agreement (NDA) for you to sign, so I'll accept your word as an officer that anything you hear from this point goes any further. Do you accept my conditions?"

"Yes Ma'am."

"What Max gave Zegers was a copy of telephone intercepts, cell phones, between the President of the Board, and two of the board members. You were about to be railroaded out of the Marine Corps. Zegers was implicated in those calls by the President of the Board. Along with those transcripts was a notation that those calls were recorded, and that recording would be made available to the Judge Advocates Office if required."

"So, I get shit on and they get to continue their careers."

"No Karla, each individual involved will find the main gate. They'll never see another promotion and will be asked to retire. That's not great comfort to you, but if the Commandant fired all of them at one time, the fall out could be nasty."

"That's what Colonel Conley meant about the politics."

"Yes, Michael said you one of his best, if not the best student he ever trained, and would really like to have you in his squadron, possibly as the Executive Officer."

"You know Colonel Conley?"

Max smiled,

"Karla, I was the Aide de Camp to General Megan Conley, Michael's mother."

"Sandra, chows on its way." Taylor commented from his position.

"Sit Pat and no more talk about this subject. We have other things to talk about." Sandra commented.

Dinner was served and as Karla was taking a bite of her salad, Sandra brought up the other thing she mentioned.

"Karla, how would you like to get back into a cockpit?"

"Sandra, I just might kill for that chance."

"Then come and work for me. I need an Aide, and it'll give you a chance to fly, maybe not in Cheyenne's, but fly."

Karla looked at both General's before responding.

"Both of you are still on active duty?"

"Karla, at this point I give you a choice. Come be my Aide, fly with Oak Leaf's on your uniform. I can't say any more than that at this time."

"When do I have to make my decision General?"

"You have until dessert is over."

They had not even gotten to the dessert stage of dinner when Karla commented on her decision.

"Sandra, General Grainger, I accept your offer."

Sandra put her fork down, rinsed the food in her mouth down with a glass of water, then pulled a cell phone from her bag beside her chair. She hit speed dial and waited. Karla could not hear the other side of the conversation, but what she heard interested her.

"Conrad, she took my offer. I leave the rest in your capable hands. (pause) Certainly. (pause) Thank you and have a good evening."

Karla suspected Sandra had just talked to the Commandant since his first name was Conrad.

"Captain, just go about your present duties and soon everything will come together. Until we have an NDA to cover your new assignment, there will be no more discussion. Relax, you'll learn this is just policy, and the reason for it."

"No problem Sandra, as long as I get back into a cockpit, I'll sit naked on a red ant hill if necessary."

Everyone at the table laughed at her comment and the rest of dinner was taken up with talk about Karla's childhood and college. When the subject of Taylor's possible engagement came up, Karla knew he was off the market. She quietly laughed at herself for considering another relationship so soon after dumping Ron, but Taylor was an attractive man, and certainly more of a man than Ron could ever be.

The next morning, Karla was instructed to be at the Commandant's Office at ten. She left his office fifteen minutes later with the Gold Oak Leaf's of a Major on her uniform, and orders in her hands to report to the Twenty-First Special Operations Group at the earliest possible date.

Karla cleared her desk and went home to pack. She had only been home for less than twenty minutes before there was a knock on her door. She opened it to find Pat Taylor in civilian clothes and five other men with him. He said they were there to pack her things up and ship them to the Twenty-First. He also took her cell phone advising it would be returned at their final destination.

She shortly discovered that besides Taylor, three of the other men were men she had lifted out of the firefight in Ecuador. By eight that evening, she found herself on a Gulfstream VII out of Andrews Air Force Base with just her luggage heading into the unknown.

Culture Shock

For Karla, the trip to Texas was interesting and enjoyable as she was invited to the cockpit of the Gulfstream, and was able to not only sit in the Co-Pilot's seat for an hour, she was given control of the aircraft as the Pilot gave her instructions.

She discovered that even though both pilots were wearing civilian clothing, they were retired Air Force pilots who had flown dignitaries all over the world. Karla thought that this might not be the cockpit of an attack helicopter, but it would certainly be better than flying a desk.

Karla was puzzled when they landed in Texas to find what some might consider an abandoned airfield late in the evening with very few lights to give her an idea of where she was at. The man who greeted her as she got off the aircraft was an Army Sergeant Major named Gonzales, who told her he was the Group's Sergeant Major, he then loaded her into a four-wheel drive ATV with her luggage and drove off into the darkness.

From what she could see as they drove through the darkness were non-descript buildings with no set pattern. Of the lights displayed on the buildings, one had a red light and a small sign stating it was the Canteen. Less than a minute later he turned down into what was a ramp taking them underground and parked. It was obvious from appearance this was a medical facility with several ATV's parked out of the way with litters on them, basically field ambulances.

He introduced her to a female doctor who was not wearing any rank on her white lab coat, but was introduced as Major Cummings. Major Cummings was warm and friendly and told her to call her Sue. Karla was taken back to an area where there were individual apartments and shown her temporary quarters. The Sergeant Major told her that in the morning, she would go through a complete physical. He then showed her the cafeteria and told her it was open twenty-four/seven, and all she had to do was sign the roster to eat. Drinks were not accounted for so no need to sign in for that.

He told her she was restricted to the hospital until she was read into the system, and briefed on how the Group operated. When she asked when that would occur, he told her as soon as her physical was complete. Karla was also told she would be in Bungalow Five as soon as her things arrived.

Uniform for tomorrow would be PT clothing for the physical, the digitals unless otherwise specified. Since she hadn't had much to eat, she went to the cafeteria and found they would make her anything she wanted. Karla ordered a Rueben Sandwich and found it was one of the best she had every eaten.

As she was sitting in the cafeteria, she listened to the few people taking a late dinner. Some were in civilian clothing and others were in a mixture of uniforms, some dirty as if they just came out of the field. What began to confuse her was that even if they had rank showing on their uniforms, a Sergeant might refer to an officer by their first name.

Marine Aviation was known to be looser than the regular Corps, but never that loose. Then she realized that at no time had the Sergeant Major saluted her as per protocol. And after working at HQMC, where she could not walk across the parking lot without being saluted a dozen times, this felt different.

Karla went to bed thinking that she'd be glad once she could get back behind the controls of an aircraft, any aircraft where she felt in control, instead of being controlled, which she admitted to herself was her one real fault. As much as she enjoyed being a Marine, she hated that she had limited control of her own life, except when in the air. Karla accepted flight restrictions as being for her, her craft, and any passenger's safety. And she had certainly broke several in Ecuador.

The physical she received was more in depth than her required flight physical. She had maintained an exercise regimen while at HQMC to ensure she was ready to return to flight status when available. It threw her off when Sue Cummings asked about her sexual activities and her birth control. When Karla questioned that aspect, Doctor Cummings told her that would all be explained in her briefing, plus knowledge of type birth control would ensure that their pharmacy would have her prescription on hand.

Again, she noticed that the Corpsman would refer to Doctor Cummings as Sue, instead of her rank or position. But when Karla referred to one of them as Corpsman, she was told they were a Medic, not a Corpsman. It then dawned on Karla that Doctor Cummings was a Major, not a Lieutenant Commander meaning she had to be Army, or Air Force.

Karla was told to return to her quarters and change. She was free to have breakfast, and someone would come collect her up when it was time for her briefing. She changed then went to the cafeteria for breakfast, and again watched and listen to the conversation of those around her. Everyone was friendly with her, greeting her by her rank, but no one sat at her table. She also noted that there were more men than women in the cafeteria which wasn't too surprising since the balance on active duty was in favor towards men.

A hard-looking Marine Gunny came to her table and said his name was DeMello, and he was to take her to the Bunker for her briefing once she finished breakfast. She looked at the remains of the vegetable omelet on her plate and as tasty as it was, she had enough.

DeMello walked her over to what appeared to be a covered parking area, then down a ramp into a large room, larger than the parking area above it. It was nearly wall to wall desks with two or more computer monitors on them with people working at each station. The place looked like organized chaos with uniforms from every branch of service, plus some in civilian clothing.

She was led down a hallway that zig-zagged, so you could not see the end of it. There were offices along the hallway with small signs beside the doors, but she did not hesitate to read them. When the hallway straightened out, there was a closed door with a sign advertising it as the Conference Room.

DeMello ushered her into the room and allowed her to enter by herself, then closed the door behind her. Inside the room was a large conference table capable of sitting over a dozen people, but the only people in the room was the Sergeant Major and a black, female in Army ACU's with a Silver Oak Leaf on her uniform.

"Come in and take a seat Major, we have much to discuss." Instructed the black officer.

Karla took a seat across from the Lieutenant Colonel as a piece of paper was passed over to her with an ink pen on top of it. Karla knew what this was without reading it, but still took the time to scan the document before signing. It was her Non-Disclosure Agreement. Once signed, the Colonel started the briefing.

"Major Welch, my name is Gloria Garcia. I know you have met Sergeant Major Gonzales already. My job here is two-fold. I'm the Operations Officer for the Twenty-First and I have a Special Ops team. Gunny DeMello, who escorted you here is my number two on that team."

"Sergeant Major Gonzales is our weapons training specialist and oversees most of the training within the Group that takes place outside of the Bunker. In case you are wondering, you are in the Bunker, which is also headquarters for the Twenty-First."

Gloria went on to give a basic history lesson on the Twenty-First which caught Karla off guard since it was originally formed under General Megan Conley after the California Insurrection by President Philpot using the system against itself.

Karla stayed quiet until Gloria finished her briefing, not knowing which question to ask first.

"Colonel, the way I interpret your briefing is that basically the Twenty-First does not exist."

"Correct Major. To make us known beyond the very few people who do know about us would destroy our effectiveness. Have you ever heard of the Tiger Lily?"

"Certainly Ma'am, I think everyone has. I've even read the book and seen the movie. What does that have to do with the Twenty-First?"

"Megan Conley is the original Tiger Lily. A name she adopted while she was still working for the CIA before she transferred to the Marines. Sandra Grainger carries that call sign now."

"I understood that the Tiger Lily was a mercenary, an assassin. Am I wrong?"

"She's never been a mercenary, but in most cases, assassination is our specialty. Before you get upset, we have strict controls on who and how we remove the enemies of the country, or allies of this country. In most cases we are the last resort, often staving off war by our actions. We have also prevented the downfall of this country by removing enemies of the state. The last President knew of our existence and tried once to use us to remove what he considered a political threat. He learned we do not play his political games. The current President does not know about us, and we intend to keep it that way."

"But how can someone like myself, a Marine on active service be transferred here as if this was a normal command?"

"Because we are listed deep inside SOCOM. Granted we are separate from SOCOM, but the SOCOM Commander knows about us as does the MARSOC Commander, and if their people cannot accomplish the mission, they will refer it to us. If we feel we cannot accomplish that mission, we turn it back to them without prejudice. Any contact you have with people outside of this command will only know that you are in SOCOM which covers a vast assortment of units or groups."

"Colonel you said you had a team. Is that a Special Ops team?"

"Yes Major, it is actually considered a Black Ops team. Have you ever heard of the Black Orchid?"

"Yes, who hasn't heard of the Black Orchid. Are you saying you are the Black Orchid?"

"Yes, I am the Black Orchid. Major, this is not the path I chose when I joined the Army and was trained to be an Intelligence officer, but it is one I have accepted as a need to protect the people of our country, and the people of this world."

"Then what is my part to be in all of this? I mean this does not seem to be a place where an Aide de Camp is required."

"You're correct. Karla, you are here because the Commandant did not wish to lose you and your talents because a group of men decided that a talented pilot and proven warrior should not be flying attack helicopters."

"The Commandant?"

"Yes Karla, he could not directly influence your path because of politics. He must stay as neutral as possible at this time, especially since he is up for consideration as the next Chief of the Joint Chiefs. So, he contacted us, and we contacted Michael once we discovered the connection between the two of you.

Michael is nearly untouchable since he is the son of two Marine legends, and he understands how the game is played."

"So where does this put me? I mean even if I get to fly twice the hours as I was getting, what good is it going to do as far as a career in the Corps is concerned?"

"It's simple. Your fight records will be kept up to date along with your Service Records. When and if you return to active service, your records will reflect all of that information, except it will show you to have been working on classified projects for SOCOM. No one can dispute those records. Any certifications on additional aircraft will be fully documented and valid."

Karla sat for a long time just thinking about what she had just been told. None of this made sense to her. In order to advance her, to in a sense protect her from people who did not believe in allowing women to actively engage in combat, she would be working for the most elite group of warriors in the DOD. Allowing women in combat positions was an argument that had gone on for decades, with women being accepted in combat positions for years, then removed only to be returned. It was a roller coaster of events, and now it had taken a downturn.

"Alright Colonel Garcia, what's the game plan?"

"We already know you are certified on nearly a dozen types of aircraft, so what we would like to do is build a Valkyrie team around you."

"What's a Valkyrie Team?"

Gloria went on to explain that Valkyrie Teams were teams made up of women, who were used for intelligence gathering and when needed to support active operations without engaging the target or the targets support. She went on to explain that often their contact with a target was acceptable to a point if required, but sexual contact with the target or target support/assets was forbidden as a method of gaining information regardless how vital that information might be to the mission.

Gloria explained that the Sergeant Major oversaw all training within the Group and with certain exceptions scheduled all training. Those exceptions were in her hands and based upon the Sergeant Major's recommendations. Karla then asked what her next step was to be if she accepted a team. The Sergeant Major told her that first she would go through a physical fitness test based upon their requirements, not the Corps. Then she would be tested on the pistol range to determine the type and amount of additional training she would receive in preparation for building a team. Also, when she was ready, she would go through Fort Benning's Parachute School to get jump qualified as part of mission requirements of the Valkyries.

"What if I decide that I do not wish to be a Valkyrie? What then?"

"We'll keep our agreement with the Commandant and you will get the flight training and hours required as you work in our Intelligence section pushing paper. But you will also escort General Grainger, Sandra, from time to time, so others will see you as her aide."

"When do I have to decide?"

"Sandra and Max are not here at the moment, and are not scheduled back for a week. You will have that time to determine your path. But one thing that is fixed, and that is the physical and weapons qualifications. Even the personal within the main part of this Bunker are required to maintain those same standards, and as long as you are a member of this command, you will train to meet those standards. Are we clear on this?"

"Yes Colonel, we are. Now may I ask about living arrangements? I understand I will have a bungalow. How is that handled as far as my quarter's allowance is concerned?"

The Sergeant Major answered that question.

"Major, your quarters will cost you one half of your quarters allowance which means you keep the other half. Also, our supply will take care of keeping your pantry and fridge stocked so you will not have to leave the Compound to purchase food. Unless you request something exotic, all food supplied to your bungalow is included in the cost of living in the bungalow. We also have a weekly maid service available at an additional cost of twenty-dollars a month. They only clean the bungalow. They do not do your dishes, wash your clothes, or make your bed."

It was further explained to her that she could eat at the Hospital's cafeteria or the cafeteria in the Bunker at no additional charge. She was then told about the Canteen where she could eat or have a drink which she could either pay for or run a monthly tab. All personal were restricted to the amount of drinks they could consume at any night to prevent being unable to work the next day. Karla was then told that rank within the compound only applied to duty assignment unlike the regular services.

What caught her attention was that within the Canteen, there was no rank and it was allowable for Enlisted and Officers to intermix. There were no prohibitions on relations between the ranks or sexes as long as they did not disrupt the operations and functioning of this command. In time she would understand why this philosophy was accepted here when it would be forbidden elsewhere.

Karla was told to prepare a list of food stuffs and turn it in to Chief Mosby at Supply when she draws her equipment and weapons. The Sergeant Major said he would pick her up at zero five thirty the next morning for her physical fitness test, then later in the morning, they would be on the pistol range to test her level of competence with a handgun.

Before the meeting ended, she was told her car and things should be at the Compound late in the afternoon since the team bringing her things were driving straight through, changing drivers at fuel stops. She would be notified when they arrived, so she could supervise how her bungalow would be set up. Any additional furniture she felt she needed she could request through Supply.

As she was leaving the Conference Room the Sergeant Major made one final comment.

"Major Welch, because of the nature of our work, and because of how our teams are constructed which you will learn at a later date, we do not waste the energy saluting except for formal ceremonies, which are rare, or to the even rarer visiting officer. So, do not get your panties in a wad if an enlisted person does not salute you while you are walking around the Compound."

"Thank you, Sergeant Major, I suppose this also applies to enlisted referring to officers by their given names?"

"Major, the relationships between the personal here is near family like. Everyone depends on the other and trust must be built between them. No one here will take offense if you desire to only be addressed by your rank, but in time you will discover why the other manner works for us."

"And what do they call you Sergeant Major?"

"I'm known as Pecos which goes back to my Delta Force days, but Gloria here never calls me anything but Michael, my given name."

Karla smiled as she opened the door to leave.

"Thank you, Michael."

She exited hearing Gloria laughing and the Sergeant Major chuckling. Outside the door she found Gunny DeMello waiting for her.

"What now Gunny?"

"I'm to take you to Supply to get outfitted, then I'll show you around the Compound, so you know where things are located. We'll also go by Commo and get you one of our cell phones and instructions on how to use it. Your phone will be returned to you with after Pat turns in it to Commo and they insure it cannot be traced. In case no one has told you, be very careful of what you say to your parents when you call them. One never knows who is listening."

Karla thought about what Sandra Grainger told her about the document Max had given Zegers about cell phone transcripts. This was something she had to remember.

At Supply, DeMello helped her size and fit her equipment vest and body armor, then the placement of the difference things she would carry in and on the vest. There was a drop leg holster for her Sig P320 which had an extended barrel for a silencer. She was unfamiliar with the Sig MPX carbine she was issued, but liked the feel of it over the XM-177A2 she was issued in the Marines.

At Commo she was issued what looked like her own cell phone only to discover it had hidden talents. It was encrypted unless she authorized an unencrypted call. It had twice the battery life as a standard cell phone and it came with a recharger pack for recharging in the field. DeMello helped her carry her ammunition cans to her quarters, then left her to her own means for the rest of the day.

Karla was surprised when all of her magazines were loaded, including the ones she was to put in her weapons. When she asked about this, DeMello said everyone carried a loaded weapon at all times since General Conley was shot by a government agent assigned to her team as the General was sitting at her desk as her team was investigating the assassination of President Mansfield.

She took lunch in the cafeteria and had a nurse sat down at her table. Jennifer was her name and she was easy going and open about some aspects of relations within the Compound. She explained that the men who visited the Canteen would be polite and respectful of the females there because they understood the females controlled their own sexual desires.

Karla came to understand that on any given night she could pick and choose her playmates as long as it did not interfere with operations. But if she decided to play musical beds too often, it would come to the attention of Lieutenant Colonel Garcia which would not be a pleasant experience. It was during this conversation that Karla learned that Gloria was a widow, whose husband was killed during an operation that she was leading against a rogue U.S. Congressman.

She also learned there was a library and video selection in the hospital that she could take advantage of and went to examine the possibilities. She found a romantic mystery that she had never read and signed it out, then returned to her quarters and decided reading would be a good way to kill time before her things arrived.

Karla had just sat down for an early dinner with book in hand when DeMello showed up to tell her that her belongings had arrived. She could take her time eating then come over to the Bungalow to supervise how she wanted it set up. DeMello stayed with her, then helped her move her things was the hospital apartment to her Bungalow. By eight that evening, her apartment was set up and she just stretched out on her couch and read until ten, then went to bed.

The PT Test the next morning was grueling compared to the Marine Corps PT test she took yearly. But she was not alone in taking the test as there were four other females being tested. Two were computer techs from the Bunker, one was a nurse and the fourth was from Commo. During the test she learned that this test was taken twice a year and the other women were taking their semi-annual test and it had been postponed for a week, so Karla would not be alone in taking it.

There was a minor break in testing and Karla was standing off to the side, waiting her turn. She noticed that Gunny DeMello and another man was standing across the testing area from her, and it seemed every time she looked at DeMello, he was looking at her. Karla was dressed in dark blue Yoga pants with issue Female PT shorts over them, and a black sports bra under Marine issue black t-shirt. At first, she thought something was showing, but everything was properly fit.

One of the women moved beside Karla and introduced herself.

"Major, I'm Carol, I work in the hospital as an Emergency Room Nurse."

"Hi Carol, just call me Karla."

"Thank you, Karla. May I ask you a somewhat personal question?"

"You can ask, how I answer is another thing."

Carol chuckled.

"Fair enough. What is your preference in the bedroom?"

Karla had to fight from giving Carol a hard look as she was still watching DeMello watching her.

"I prefer whiskers between my thighs, not soft lips. You?"

"I go both ways, but as much fun one is, I do prefer the whiskers. So, I won't waste your time in that aspect, but don't worry, there are plenty of whiskers here to keep you happy."

Before she could respond, Karla was called forward to take this part of the test. The test had several elements she had never seen or had been tested on before, and she struggled to do what was required for those elements of the test.

When they lined up to start the three-mile run, Carol told Karla to pace herself, she'd need all her strength to complete the run. Karla did not understand what Carol meant, but held her pace down and ran with the other women as a group. When they hit the first mile marker, they stopped and were required to do ten push-ups, then ten set-ups before continuing. At the two-mile mark was a rock climbing wall.

Karla thought the wall was just along the running path, but found out she had to climb the ten-meter wall, then climb down the cargo net on the other side before completing the final mile. This wall was not as steep as some she had climbed, but it was still steep enough to cause major injury since there were not safety harness. There were heavy pads at the base, but bouncing off the hand-holds on the way down if someone slipped would cause injury, plus they all went up at the same time, one following another.

She got over the wall behind the others and down the net, then had to hustle to catch up to them for the final mile. Her body was aching from the long physical testing, now this. Karla downed a full bottle of water as she tried to relax after the run. She knew she had slipped a bit in her physical training while in D.C., but not that much. She moved over to speak to Carol.

"Carol, if you non-deployed women take this test, what is the test for the Valkyries?"

"Same test Karla, and we can be deployed. The only married personal are exempt from being deployed, and they still take the same test. Gloria, Colonel Garcia designed this test, and takes it quarterly. She has set a high standard, and expects us to meet it."

Karla could only nod her understanding as she started walking in a large circle to keep her legs from stiffening up. She had made two circles before Sergeant Major Gonzales approached her.

"Major Welch, it's a short walk back to your Bungalow. Go home and get cleaned up and something to eat. I'll pick you up in about ninety minutes for the range. Full gear minus helmet today. This includes your carbine even if you do not fire it today. Any questions Major?"

"Yeah, how did I do on the PT Test?"

"Your scores are not fully tabulated yet. Right now, worry about your range testing. Colonel Garcia will give you the results of your testing later today."

"Alright then. I'll see you in eighty-nine minutes."

Karla got home and stood under the hot water in her shower until it began to turn cold. She fixed an egg sandwich, chasing it with a glass of milk and two Aleve. Once she was dressed, she sat out on the small porch with a bottle of water and her book as she waited to the Sergeant Major.

When they arrived on the range, Karla noticed that DeMello and the other man was there also. She finally got a good look at the other man. Besides being clean shaved and wearing a non-descript Khaki uniform, there was no indication of rank or a name tag to identify him. He was wearing dark, wrap around glasses, and yet she felt as if he was disrobing her with his eyes.

The Sergeant Major gave her a concise explanation of how the range was set up and operated. He gave her a short demonstration of how the targets operated then allowed her three magazines to become familiar with the pistol before reloading them and processing through the actually course of fire.

She liked the Sig P320, but the threaded barrel and sights were different from what she normally qualified with. Karla wore a Pistol Sharpshooter Badge on her uniform, but this targeting system was so different she had no idea how she had performed, but she knew she left a lot of targets standing that she felt she should have hit.

46

As she was policing her brass, she noticed that DeMello and the other man had left. She was putting the last of her brass in a bucket when the Sergeant Major walked up to her.

"Time to go Major."

"How did I do Sergeant Major?"

"Actually, better than I figured. You aviation types are not noted for your skill with a handgun. Now you have the rest of the day off until sixteen hundred. From now on, do not leave your quarters in uniform without your side arm."

"Even if I go to the Canteen in uniform?"

"Even there. Major, it is so you will become used to wearing it, not because you are in danger inside the compound."

"Okay, that makes sense, I think. What happens at sixteen hundred?"

"You'll meet with Colonel Garcia and she will explain your test scores, and what needs to be done to improve on them. Major, this has nothing to do with taking a team, but being capable of responding in a manner which all members of this command is trained to do. This not so much for your own protection, but the protection of those you will serve with."

"Thank you, Sergeant Major. Let me take a quick look to see if I missed any stray brass, then I'll be ready to go."

Karla washed her face and hands once she got home, then picked up her book and went to the Bunker's cafeteria for a late lunch. As she was picking at a Seafood salad and reading the book, she caught DeMello entering the cafeteria. He only filled his travel mug with tea, nodded a greeting to her, then left. Karla smiled to herself and continued with her lunch.

At sixteen hundred hours, she found herself in Colonel Garcia's office with the Sergeant Major and the unknown man from the test and range. That individual just stood off in the corner in a relaxed posture as Gloria briefed Karla on her test results.

"Karla, you are in good physical condition for someone who has been flying a desk for the past year, but we still need to improve on it. There are several places in the physical fitness test that you passed on margin. Now as far as your pistol qualification scores, comparing today's scores with the Marine Corps standards, you qualified as a Pistol Sharpshooter which is already your current qualification. We need to improve those scores also."

"Colonel Garcia, a few of those exercises on the physical fitness test was unknown to me, and I worked hard to do them properly in the time given. But I have to admit I am surprised I did as well as I did on the pistol range."

"Karla, don't worry too much about how you did this morning, in fact you did better than we expected. In time you will find both the physical test and range scores go up with training. Now the gentleman standing in the corner is Colin Berman, he is a retired Navy Master Chief and a SEAL. He will be your chief trainer, working on your physical improvements, plus your shooting skills. Now this might seem draconian, but once you leave this office, he controls your life here with the Group until your scores improve to our standards. He sets your schedule unless the Sergeant Major or myself adjusts it for our own plans for you."

"So basically, I'm back in the Basic Course again?"

"Not really Major. I might push you hard to get things accomplished, but it does not accomplish anything to run you into the ground." Berman spoke from his position in the corner.

"Thank you, Master Chief." Karla replied.

"Karla, one other thing. Your physical condition is already good enough for us to send you to the Parachute school. The next class is in three weeks, and you will attend that class. Colin will incorporate several aspects of that school into your physical training to give you a head start there. Pay close attention to his instruction and you'll find jump school easier than most do. Do you have any questions?"

"When do we start?" Was Karla's response.

"Tomorrow morning at zero five hundred." Colin answered.

"Karla, until then you are free to do whatever you like. Unless you have any other questions, you are dismissed." Gloria instructed.

"No other questions at this time Colonel."

As Karla stood, Colin stepped over and opened the door for her. He used his left hand and Karla noticed a wedding ring on that hand. She just smiled and thanked him, then left the Bunker for her quarters. Once again, she had little control of her life, but she reminded herself, she accepted her situation at dinner with the General's, and it was beginning to be a major improvement over pushing paper at HQMC.

As she was eating dinner at the hospital, the nurse, Jennifer came to sit at her table as she ate her own meal.

"Major, this might sound like gossip between us girls, but the word is that you are heterosexual which is fine. This is only to let those who go both ways know not to waste their time. Now that does not mean they won't be friendly, and they might even ask you to dance, but will not make any move on you out of respect for your choice. I hope I have not offended you with my comments."

"No Jennifer, you have not. If I may ask, what are your preferences?"

"I prefer men. But I'm not against sleeping with a woman. It's not that I'm actually bi-sexual, but I am very selective about the men I sleep with, and even more so with a woman."

"Is everyone so open and honest here?"

"Major, the work we do for this country depends on each of us, even those of us just in support, being honest with the others. Each time a team deploys, there is a chance one or more of them will return in a body bag. I hope that makes sense to you."

"Jennifer, as a pilot, I had to trust my crew chief and the mechanics that kept my bird flying. I had to trust my observer/gunner to do the job as he trusted me to get him into a good firing position, and not to get him killed doing so. So how about you call me Karla, instead of Major all the time."

"Thank you, Karla, By the way, I'm an Air Force Captain. You'll find that all of the nurses are officers in various services."

"I figured that much. So, what is there to do around here after hours?"

"We are not restricted to the Compound, but the bars in the small towns nearby are not places we females can go without being hassled by the cowboys. Waco is the nearest large city, but again, it is not a good place for the same reasons, plus if you go off base, you have to report any sexual activity and be tested. You'll find that everyone here is tested monthly even if we never leave the Compound. This ensures our nighttime activities do not create a health problem, especially for the Ops Teams."

"What about this Canteen I keep hearing about?"

Jennifer explained how the Canteen worked to including the restrictions on consuming alcohol. Rationing made sense in that no one went to work the next day hung over. Jennifer then invited Karla to the Canteen for a beer later that evening. Karla accepted her invite.

Karla found the Canteen an interesting place with an atmosphere that was warm and friendly. There were no waiters or waitresses to deal with the customers, so if you wished a drink, you went to the bar, gave them you name and ordered your drink.

She sat at a table with Jennifer and two other females, both who worked in the Bunker as computer techs. She found both of the techs were enlisted, one from the Navy and the other from the Army. It was a friendly conversation as they asked what she did, and they seemed very interested in her flying attack helicopters.

All during the evening, men came over and invited the women to dance. At one point, the Navy tech came back to the table, smiled and told everyone to have fun, then left with the man she had danced with. Jennifer explained that it was on the dance floor that couples came together for a night of fun in a bed. But she could dance with a dozen men without that aspect, and she had to make the move as the men would never push themselves on to a female. She had to want to go to bed, and she had the right to pick and choose her playmate, the men only accepted their part in this situation.

Karla finally danced with two men before DeMello entered the Canteen and took a seat with four other men at a table. His seat was not where he could look directly at Karla, but from time to time he could turn her way for a moment, then back to his friends. Karla asked Jennifer about him.

"Pete? He is an interesting man. He has probably turned down more women than he has slept with. Some thought he was gay at first, but he has proved that wrong according to a few of the girls."

"Have you slept with him?"

"No Karla, I like Pete, but something about him tells me to keep him in the friendly category, not the lover file. But two of the men he is sitting with have enjoyed what I have to offer. But tonight, I'm sleeping alone."

51

Karla sat for a bit then decided she needed another drink. She excused herself and went to the bar. As she waited for her cocktail, she looked at DeMello. Once she had her drink, she walked over to his table and stepped in between him and the man to his left. DeMello looked up at her.

"Gunny, I was told if I wanted to learn how to do the Texas Two-Step, you were the man to teach me that dance. How about the next time a song comes up to fit that profile, you teach me how to do the Two-Step?"

"Sure Major, but I'm not sure I'm the right man for it, but we can give it a try."

"Call me Karla." With that she went back to the table with Jennifer who was smiling at her.

Two dances later, DeMello came to her table and offered his hand to her. Out on the dance floor, he chuckled within the first couple of steps into the dance.

"Karla, you already know how to Two-Step. What's this about?"

"Gunny, I notice you keep looking at me, and this is as good a place as any to ask you why?"

"Please call me Pete. Now as far as looking at you, from the first time I saw you, I told myself I knew you. Or knew someone that looked like you. It took me awhile, but I have figured that out."

"What did you figure out Pete?"

"If you had black hair, dark eyebrows, and brown eyes, you would be an exact copy of an actress from the black and white era of film. That's what threw me off, your red hair and green eyes."

"Who do I look like?"

"Hedy Lamar."

"I'll have to look her up then."

They danced the rest of the dance in silence, and Karla went back to her table without any suggestion of further contact. She danced with another man from the table later, then left alone with DeMello watching her as she walked out of the Canteen.

She looked up Hedy Lamar on her computer, then compared her own face with a hand mirror at the computer. Yes, there was a similarity between them, but she felt Hedy was certainly much more beautiful.

Karla went to bed thinking that even though much of what she had been told about how the Twenty-First functioned, it was still so very different from what she was used too.

Falling is Easy, Landing is Difficult

For the next three weeks. Colin Berman pushed her hard in the gym and on the track to improve her physical strength. On the range he was another person, using a soft voice and gentle hand as he corrected her firing positions, grip on her handgun and mental timing during firing.

In the second week of training, he had her jumping off a table into a sand pile leaning how to properly land doing the Parachute Landing Form. There was also a small tower from which she jumped while in a parachute harness and slide down a cable to a landing, also learning how to properly land.

She often went to the Canteen during that time with a slight limp from the bruised hip or leg from the landing practice and danced with any man who asked, and even danced with Jennifer once just for fun. If DeMello was in the Canteen, she would have to ask him to dance, but never took it further than the dance floor.

Her physical form was firming up as she pushed herself in the gym, gaining muscle mass while removing body fat. Her scores on the pistol range had improved to the point that Berman had her firing her carbine to learn how it functioned and fired.

The night before she left for Jump School, she danced with DeMello twice, before going home alone. The next morning, DeMello was at the air strip when she flew off in a twin-prop aircraft for Fort Benning.

Karla found herself to be the highest-ranking officer in her class at Jump School, which put additional responsibilities on her. After the training that Berman had given her, she found the school was not as difficult as many made it out to be.

During the second week of Jump School, she took a classmate, an Army Captain, to bed for that one night, and never ventured further than that as she progressed through the course.

54

She bruised her hip bad enough she was sent to the hospital for examination when she landed on a rock during her third qualifying jump. The Army doctor wanted to put her on a training hold, but she told him she was making the next two jumps regardless of what he said. He gave her a shot of Cortisone in the hip, then a prescription for a non-narcotic pain med and sent her back to the school.

She made her next two jumps spending the nights in a whirlpool to take as much of the pain out of her hip as possible. When she arrived back at the Compound, once she had put her things away, she reported to the Hospital and reported that she had slept with one man for one night and he had used a condom. Blood was taken as was a urine sample, then she was told to behave herself until the results came back.

Captain Mattis, the Navy doctor who was in command of the hospital examined her hip, to include having an MRI done on it before she was released to limited duty to give the hip time to heal. The MRI only showed deep bruising with no apparent damage to the joint.

That night she went to the Canteen and dance with three men before going to bed alone. The next morning after a short workout, giving consideration to her hip, she was fixing a light breakfast at home when the phone rang. It was Jennifer at the hospital advising her that her blood and urine tests came back negative, so she was free to enjoy which ever male victim she chose. Karla laughed and told Jennifer she would see her at the Canteen tonight.

On the range that day she began doing small movements up and down the firing line, working her hip trying to work the stiffness out of it. Berman tried to make her stop since to him, she was missing shots because she was feeling the pain in her hip. She told him how else was she to get past the pain and hit her targets if she was in the field if she did not take advantage of her situation. He conceded to her position and continued with that days training.

She was on the range an hour longer than normal, and her hip was causing her a lot of grief, but her scores improved back to her last set before her injury then improved on them as she fought through the pain. When she started picking up her brass, she found she could barely get up from being on her knees until a strong hand was offered to her. She looked up to see DeMello standing beside her.

"Thanks Pete. I guess I'm not as in good a shape as I figured."

"Karla, Colin called the Colonel and told her what you were doing out here. I am the messenger here. You will slow your ass down, or the Colonel will order you to the hospital until your hip completely heals. Do you accept this coming from me, or do I have to haul your ass in front of Colonel Garcia?"

"No Pete, I accept those orders as given."

"Good, now I'll help you police your brass, then I'm taking you back to your quarters where you will change clothes, then to the gym where you will soak in a whirlpool. This is from me, not the Colonel."

"I won't argue with you Pete. I guess I'm just being stubborn."

"Let me tell you a little secret. Gloria took a hit in her left hip during our very first team operation. Large splinters from a tree she was standing by that was hit by incoming fire embedded in her hip. She led us out of a bad situation while wounded till we found a place to be taken out by an Osprey. She knows what it is like to have a hip wound, so she is just taking care of you."

"I never doubted that she wasn't Pete. Let's get this done so I can get into that whirlpool."

DeMello took her home and stayed outside the bungalow as Karla changed. She took the pain meds she received at Benning accordance to prescription as she stood nude in her bathroom. Her entire hip was nearly black from the bruise and she could not ignore the pain in it. She looked in her dresser for something to wear in the whirlpool and realized she did not had anything but bikini's. She picked the most modest bottom and then a modest top before carefully pulling on a pair of satin shorts, then a t-shirt to cover her torso.

Karla was wondering as she rode to the gym what DeMello was going to think about her body since he would have to help her into the whirlpool. What she found out once in the whirlpool room was that DeMello had called the hospital and a female Corpsman was there to assist her into the tub, and would stay with her to help her out later.

This proved to be a blessing in that a combination of the heat from the water soothing her aches, and the meds she had taken put her to sleep in the tub. The Corpsman prevented her from slipping down under the water and held her until she was awakened to get out thirty minutes later.

The Corpsman assisted her in getting dressed, then helped DeMello take her back to the Bungalow, then into bed after she got her bikini off, dried off again, then covered with a t-shirt. Once the Corpsman advised DeMello that Karla was decent and in bed under covers, he entered the bedroom to speak with her.

"Karla, did you take anything for pain?"

She was groggy, but could answer.

"Yes, docs at Benning gave me some pain meds. They're in the bathroom."

He went in and found the bottle on the sink counter.

"How many did you take Karla?"

"One. No wait, I may have taken two. I don't remember."

DeMello turned to the Corpsman and handed her the bottle of meds.

"Lucy, get these to Sue Cummings ASAP, and find out everything you can about them. I'll stay here and watch the Major until you return."

DeMello went for a kitchen chair and sat just outside her bedroom looking in on Karla as she settled into a deep sleep. Twenty minutes later, Lucy returned with help and a litter. DeMello just carefully picked Karla up and laid her on the litter, then assisted carrying her to the hospital and into one of the emergency examination rooms. He stood back as they took blood and stepped out of the room as she had a catheter inserted to draw off urine for testing.

Gloria came into the room and pulled him out to join in a conversation with Sue Cummings and Captain Mattis. Sue laid out a napkin on the counter of the nurse's station and poured out the few pills left in the bottle. To the casual observer, they looked the same. She separated them before speaking.

"This group of pills fit the prescription on the bottle. They are mild and non-habit forming. But these are very potent and habit forming."

There were over a dozen of the non-habit-forming pills on the napkin, and five of the others.

"From what I gather, I really doubt Major Welch would supplement her meds with something more powerful. Her medical records have a remark from a Doctor at flight school about her refusing pain meds for a strained muscle there. If I was a betting person, I'd say someone at Benning screwed up and mixed the pills. I would guess that these other pills were at the bottom of her bottle and she finally got to them. If she took two, she'll sleep for quite a while, but she'll be alright over all. She must have been in

58

a lot of pain to take two pills. Her MRI shows no damage, but that does not mean the nerves which pass through that region are not injured."

"What's the prognosis?" Gloria asked.

"We let that hip heal, then test her again. Once the swelling goes down in that hip, the pressure on the nerves should go away. But she is on bed rest for the next week." This was Captain Mattis answering the question.

"You're the doctor." Gloria then turned to DeMello. "Pete, please make sure her bungalow is secure."

"No problem Gloria. I didn't give her any time to clean her weapons after the range, so I'll take care of them for her. Anything else?"

"No Pete. Good call on having those meds checked. Doctors, we'll get out of your way, and thanks."

As Gloria and DeMello were walking back to the Bunker, Gloria commented on Karla's stubbornness. DeMello laughed before replying.

"Look who is talking about being stubborn!"

"What do you mean by that?"

"Well, shall we discuss your near legendary walk out of Uganda? Our first jaunt in Columbia or that trip into Thailand?"

"Okay, Okay, maybe I can be a bit stubborn at times." She paused for a moment before continuing. "So, when are you going to ask her out?"

DeMello stopped in his tracks.

"Ask who out?"

"Come on Pete, I've known you too long to not see that you are attracted to Major Welch."

"How do you figure I'm attracted to her?"

"Because in the past, if I asked you to be an errand boy for me, you'd give me grief then go do it. With her you're almost out the door before I can finish telling you what I need."

He just stood looking at Gloria before sighing then started walking again.

"Honestly I don't know. Come on, look at me, and look at her. She's drop dead gorgeous, and I look like an unmade bed."

Gloria stopped walking causing DeMello to stop with her. She reached over and gently touched his arm.

"Pete, I love you like a brother, you know that. Even without Marco's scars, he would not have been the most attractive man on the block. I doubt if I can ever explain, even to myself what attracted him to me, but I wanted him, and he accepted me. The worse that can happen is she says no, and if she does, at least you can say you tried then move on. But don't spend the rest of your life wondering what it would have been like to spend one night with her."

Neither spoke as they continued on to the Bunker.

Karla woke with a headache and dry throat, wondering where she was. She tried to move and could feel the catheter in her, then the IV in her arm.

"Be still Major."

Karla looked over to see a female in scrubs moving to her, but did not know if she was a nurse or medic.

"Who are you?"

"I'm a Corpsman, Ma'am. Let me raise your head some, and I'll help you take a drink."

The Corpsman raised the head of her bed up, then held a straw to her mouth so Karla could drink. Once she felt her throat seem to cool, she moved her head away from the straw.

"What happened?"

"Major, it looks as if you came close to overdosing on your pain meds. Not your fault Major, according to Doctor Cummings, the pharmacy at Benning mixed your meds with some that are very potent."

"How long have I been out?"

"Almost twenty hours. Now just lie still and rest. I'll go get you some Jell-O or ice cream if you'd like. Something easy on your stomach."

"I think ice cream might be good. Any flavor is fine with me. What is your name?"

"I'm Lucy, I helped you at the whirlpool yesterday, remember?"

"Oh, yes you did. Thank you, Lucy."

"I'll be right back."

Lucy left and a couple minutes later Sue Cummings entered the room.

"Karla, Lucy said you were awake. How are you feeling?"

"Hip hurts, and I feel like shit. Otherwise just grand."

Sue laughed.

"Before you ask, your hip is going to be alright. I checked your medical records and talked to the doctor at Benning that treated you there. You should have taken his advice and not made those other two jumps.   And Colin described how you were moving on the range yesterday.   You aggravated your injury and the swelling is putting pressure on the nerves that pass along your hip, causing you the pain you are feeling.   The IV we have in you is for fluids and it contains an anti-inflammatory to help reduce the swelling.   But you are on bed rest for the next seven days."

"Lucy said I nearly OD'd.   The last I remember was getting into my own bed.   How did I get here?"

"Pete DeMello.   He recognized that something wasn't right with you and had your pain meds sent over here to be checked. That's when we found out about the mix-up with them.   I ordered you brought in once I saw the mistake in case you had, or were having a reaction to them.   But everything is good as far as your lab work goes."

"I'll have to thank him.   Pete that is."

Sue raised Karla's head up some more and pointed to the far corner of the room.   Sitting on a hospital stand was a vase with a dozen, red roses.

"Where did those come from?"

"Guess."

"Pete?"

"Correct."

"Son of a gun.   That was nice of him."

"Anyway, relax and enjoy the time off if that is possible. We'll remove the IV once that bag is empty, and remove the catheter then also.   But you are not to attempt going to the toilet without someone to assist you.   You've done enough damage to that hip as it is, but by the time we release you, it should be good to go."

Lucy returned with a bowl of strawberry ice cream and helped Karla eat it by managing the spoon for her. The rest of the day for Karla was just lying in the bed, watching television. The IV was removed along with the catheter late in the afternoon.

Karla found it painful to sit up enough to feed herself at dinner time, but a male medic named Bill helped her get through that, then later Susan, a nurse helped her to the toilet, then back in bed. As she was getting into bed, a form appeared in her doorway, then quickly moved out of sight. Karla wasn't sure who it had been, because she had not been able to see through Susan. When Susan left the form reappeared.

"Pete DeMello, get you butt in here."

"I just came by to check on how you were doing."

"Why did you hide while I was getting into bed?"

"Well, just in case that fancy hospital gown you are wearing decided not to cover certain aspects of your person, I moved to give you that privacy."

Karla laughed.

"Thank you sir, and thank you for the roses. They are lovely, and I can even smell them from here. Can I ask you a favor?"

"Certainly, you can."

"My memory of yesterday is shot to hell, but I do not think I cleaned my pistol after the range. Could you bring it over, so I can take care of that?"

"Already been taken care of Karla. I cleaned it after you were secure in that bed, and I checked your MPX, just to be sure. Also, when we were told you'd be kept here for a week, I put your wet things from the whirlpool into the washer, then the dryer so they would not mildew."

Karla looked at Pete with a sly look on her face.

"So, you saw what I was wearing in the whirlpool?"

"Yes, Major Welch, and I had to remove some things from your dryer. All items are folded and on top of your dresser for you to put away when you return home, to include that piece of cloth often referred to as a bikini."

Karla laughed until she groaned as it caused her to move on the bed irritating her hip.

"Karla are you alright?"

"Pete, please do not make me laugh. I moved wrong, and my hip did not like it. And we need to get that hip back in shape, don't we?"

"Yeah, there is still a lot of training ahead Karla, plus we need to get you back in a cockpit as soon as possible."

"That's not what I was talking about Pete."

"Oh?"

"There is no way we can do the Two-Step with me laid up now is there?"

"No, I guess not. You get better and we'll have that dance."

He turned to leave.

"Pete."

"Yes Karla?"

"Sue told me what you did for me. Thank you."

"Think nothing of it. Now get your rest."

The rest of Karla's time in the hospital was taken up with watching television or reading with Lucy selecting books for her from the library. On the fifth day, another MRI was taken then Karla was given physical therapy to help loosen her stiff joints from being restricted to bed.

On the seventh day, she was given another MRI, then put on a tread mill to see how she was doing. Karla was honest that there was some discomfort in the hip, but she didn't have any actual pain as she had before. Colin Berman observed her on the tread mill and between him and Captain Mattis, they developed an exercise regimen to get her back in form without stressing her.

Mattis explained the MRI to her and told her that if that rock she had landed on had been bigger or more pointed, she would have most likely suffered a crippling injury. Berman said he had jumped into that drop zone many times and the Army tried to keep it clear of anything that might cause an injury. That rock might have been unsurfaced during a training drop of vehicles and not noticed for removal.

Karla was released from the hospital to limited duty. During her stay at the hospital, she had Lucy do some background research for her on what Pete DeMello's favorite food was. Karla was planning on inviting him to dinner at her bungalow that night. Before she could invite him, he showed up as she was preparing to leave her hospital room.

"Karla, Colonel Garcia would like you to attend dinner at her house this evening. Sandra and Max will also be there."

"Damn, I had other plans. Alright, I guess this is a duty calls situation. Now I have to ask, where does Colonel Garcia live?"

"Simple. Take the ATV that is under the canopy at your bungalow down the main road until you come to a gate. The security personal will let you through and a mile further on, you'll come to a sprawling hacienda style home. That is where Gloria lives with her son and father-in-law, Tomas.

"Gloria has a son?"

"Yeah, he's five and a hand full. But he also has better manners than some eighteen-year old's I know. And watch out for Tomas. He was on Megan Conley's Tiger Team. Tomas has a dry sense of humor, and is not bashful about making you blush."

"He was on the team that was mentioned so often in the book?"

"Yeah, he was General Conley's explosives expert."

"Thanks for the warning."

"No problem. Now the dinner is at seven, and the dress is civilian. Do not bring up any aspect of what we do here in front of Marco, Gloria's son. Any business they wish to discuss with you will be after dinner, and Marco has gone to his room."

"Okay. Thanks again."

DeMello started to leave when she stopped him.

"Pete. Unless something during this meeting changes things, would you have dinner with me tomorrow night, at my place?"

"Yes, Karla, I think I'd like that."

"Good, let's shoot for seven and I'll be in civvies, so you might as well also unless you have to work late. Your choice."

"Seven it is. Good day Karla."

"Good day Pete."

Karla had no idea how long it would take to go from her bungalow to Gloria's house, so she left early to insure she had time. She was amazed at how large it was as she parked her ATV in the front of the house. Karla was wearing slacks and a nice blouse since she was driving an ATV. When she knocked on the

66

door, it was opened by a Mexican gentleman with grey hair and mustache.

"You must be Major Welch. I'm Tomas, please come in."

Please call me Karla, Tomas. I understand you are Colonel Garcia's father-in-law."

"Yes I am. Can I get you something to drink as we wait for dinner?" He spoke as he was guiding her into the living room.

"No, I'm fine, thank you."

"Karla, you're a bit early." Gloria spoke from the dining room entrance. She was also wearing slacks and a blouse with an apron around her waist.

"I wasn't sure how far I had to travel Ma'am. The directions did not give me that information. Can I be of help?"

"No, I've got it, just rest that hip."

Tomas entertained Karla while they waited to be call into dinner. The clock on the fireplace mantle showed it was five minutes till seven when the Grainger's walked in from the back of the house. Karla stood when they entered the living room.

"Sit Karla, no need to stand here in Gloria's home." Max Grainger spoke.

"Thank you, Sir. I was not aware of the protocol tonight."

"Karla let's keep this simple, first names are less confusing." Sandra Grainger instructed.

Gloria called them to the table a minute later. Karla found herself in the middle of a large table to where everyone could look at her. She discovered that Marco, Gloria's son had already eaten and was in his room. Dinner was pork steak with vegetables and once Tomas finished his dinner, he excused himself, explaining he was going to go help Marco assemble an Erector-Set.

Sandra Grainger opened the discussion once Tomas left the room.

"Karla, until the doctor's give you an all clear, there is no need to require a decision from you concerning your assignment with the Group. Your health is more important at this time."

"Thank you, Sandra. To be honest, I was afraid this dinner was to have me make a choice."

"No, but we have arranged to borrow a couple of helicopters for you to train on once you are released back to full duty. They will be brought here along with Instructor pilots that have been vetted and cleared to come here. These are aircraft not normally found in our inventory, but can be found on foreign airfields all over the world."

"Sandra, that almost sounds like you are prepping me for a team."

"True, but it will put you back in a cockpit, get you back on flight pay, and give you training you would not normally see. These aircraft are owned by SOCOM and are used in training some of their folks."

"Well then my flight records won't look so odd then, will they?"

"No, they won't."

The rest of the meeting was taken with how a team would be built around her if she decided to go that direction. Also, the restrictions in which the Valkyrie teams worked under. Karla knew there was something deep behind the no sex with target or associates rule in gaining intelligence from the tone which Sandra used but decided this was neither the time or place to explore that reasoning.

She learned that the Valkyries mission was to provide logistical support to operational teams as needed besides the obvious gathering of intelligence. This was one aspect that she could cover with her ability to fly. Karla returned to her bungalow just before ten with a better feeling for her reason for being in the Group.

The next morning, Colin put her through stretching exercises to help loosen her hip from being on bed rest without straining herself. He pushed her hard on developing greater strength in her arms with a Bow-Flew and free weights.

Later, on the pistol range, he restricted the span of targets, so she would not have much movement, if any, to tackle the course of fire. From the pistol range to the one-hundred-meter range to get more practice with her MPX.

She had lunch in the hospital cafeteria, only eating a small salad, then home to clean her weapons before straightening the house up and preparing for dinner that night. From her unpacked boxes in the spare bedroom, she took unscented candles and placed them about the house and in her bedroom.

Karla had a nice table cloth on the table and dishes set as the dinner warmed on the stove before changing into a dress that had a plunging V-neck showing her ample cleavage, and the dress was worn without a bra. She was not wearing any makeup and no perfume. If she was going to seduce Pete DeMello, it would be as she was, not something other than herself.

DeMello knocked on her door exactly at seven which made her smile. She tossed the apron she had on aside and went to the door. Opening it she saw a whole different person than a Marine Gunnery Sergeant. The man before her was wearing a dark blue suit, with a medium Blue Arrow shirt with the collar open. In his hands was a bottle of white wine and she noticed that instead of the military style watch he always wore, he had a Gold banded watch that she thought was a Rolex. She could also smell his musky aftershave.

DeMello could hardly believe that the woman who opened the door was the one who had made this date. He had trouble taking his eyes away from her bosom, which seemed larger than normal with the dress she was wearing. He could only admire what was standing in two-inch heels before him

"My God Karla, your beautiful."

"Thank you Mister DeMello. I have to say you clean up very nice yourself. Please come in, I just placed dinner on the table."

She accepted the bottle of wine from him and led him to the table. She looked at the label on the wine and noticed it was not a brand she was aware of, then handed it back to him so he could open it. He opened the bottle, poured a portion in her glass and handed it to her. She sipped it and smiled as she enjoyed the flavor.

He did not take his seat until she took hers which he assisted in her seating. Karla had prepared pasta with marinara sauce mixed with beef and mushrooms. There was a small salad for both and French bread cut in diagonal slices, buttered with garlic.

As they ate, they questioned each other about their lives. Karla discovered that Peter, his given name, was divorced with two teenage sons living with their mother in Ohio. His eldest son would start college the next year and had offers to the academy's if he desired them. Peter had married a female Marine, but when he decided to go into Recon, then the Raider's, she wanted him either back in the regular Corps or out.

Peter said the one good thing about his ex-wife was she never bad mouthed him in front of the boys and was always friendly when he went to visit. In fact, for the first two years of the divorce, she had him sleep with her whenever he visited, which caused him some difficulty in that he knew she was trying to seduce him away from the Marines.

He never slept with her after that, and she finally met and married a man who took care of the boys, and was always friendly when he visited.

She grew up in Washington, outside of Seattle, where her father worked for Boeing as an airframe assembly technician. She learned to fly when she was twelve and had her pilot's license when she was fifteen. She had graduated from the University of Washington with her degree in Aerospace Engineering, and joined the Marine Corps to be a pilot.

Karla first trained on Blackhawks and Venom utility helicopter's until she was given a chance to fly the Cheyenne. After getting her Cheyenne certificate, she cross trained on the Viper.

From there the conversation turned to music, books, and movies. It was here she found out about his comparison between her and the actress, Hedy Lamar. Peter's father was a stunt man in Hollywood, and Peter had been on many movie sets watching him practice his trade. Peter himself had a half-dozen movie credits doing minor stunts for youth actors.

Being in that environment, he came to enjoy many of the old, black and white movies which Hedy Lamar was a major player in that era. This was where he had seen Lamar's face.

Karla asked him why he joined the Marines, to which Peter replied that he knew several stunt men and a couple of actors that had been Marines and he figured on giving it a shot before possibility going into stunt work with his father. But his father was hurt on a movie and had to retire from that work while Peter was in Infantry school.

DeMello notice every time she called him by name, it was no longer Pete, but Peter. He often smiled to himself when she did that because the only people who called him Peter was his family.

Karla served up a Cherry Cheese cake for dessert with coffee. It was during dessert that Peter finally noticed that night had fallen, and the bungalow was being lit by candles except for the kitchen as he was so focused on Karla as they ate and talked.

When they both agreed diner was complete, she used a remote to turn on her stereo. Soft music consumed the bungalow as she stood and offered her hand.

"Dance with me Peter."

He stood and took her hand. Slowly they dance in the small living room until the music stopped. When the next tune began, she pulled his face down and kissed him. Karla knew from how he returned her kiss how the night would end.

When they broke the kiss, she pushed out of his embrace, then walked to her bedroom door. She unfastened the clasp behind her dress and let it fall to the floor. Peter laughed as he took his jacket off, then tossed it to the couch.

"Peter, why are you laughing?"

"Karla, I guess I was fourteen, and having fun with a young actress on a movie Dad was working on. One of the older stuntmen knew I was enjoying this girl, and she was also red headed. He told me to beware of red heads wearing black panties."

Karla looked down and realized she was wearing black, French cut panties. She pushed them down off her hips, then too her feet. She stepped out of them, then kicked them at Peter. He caught them, then tossed them over his shoulder. She laughed as she turned into her room as he followed, removing his shirt as he entered her bedroom to find her already on her bed waiting.

The night was long for them as they could never get to sleep until late, then her alarm went off reminding her she had physical training. They took a long, hot shower together which they both had to fight from ending up back in bed.

She dressed for PT while he dressed to go to his quarters and change for the day of duty. As they stood behind her closed door before leaving, she asked a favor of him.

"Peter, this is Thursday. Would you come back tomorrow night if possible?"

"Is that wise?"

"I don't care at the moment. But I have to know if what I am feeling is infatuation or reality. The only way to determine that is to continue. Lie to me and tell me you don't feel the same way."

"Karla, I can't lie, but I don't want you hurt if yours is reality, and mine is only a desire to have you."

"Then have your fill of your desires. I've been down this path before, as I was engaged while in college, but he left me when I would not follow him, instead of joining the Corps. I'm older and wiser now, and can accept what reality truly is."

"Karla, I will be here, but you must do something for me."

"Anything."

"We will eat at the Canteen, dance, and even dance with others before returning to your bed. But you will dress like a free woman. I know you must have bras that enhance those lovely breasts of yours, wear one and something that anyone seeing you will think, Pete you are one lucky bastard. Dress for yourself, but let yourself be seen, not just part of you."

"I have just the outfit Peter. Now I have to go and meet Colin in the gym."

They kissed again, then went their separate ways. DeMello wondered what he was getting himself into by agreeing to return so soon, but then again, she was the most beautiful woman he had ever slept with and she was vigorous, very skilled in and out of bed. Karla thought that he was not the largest of manhood to join with her, he was still more than enough for any woman. She had to smile at the fact he put his mustache to use in the right places, and worked hard to ensure that she was pleased with his performance.

How their relationship might end was not as important to Karla as it was to enjoy the time. To enjoy the moment. If it became more than she imagined it might, that was just sauce for the goose.

100 Percent

The Friday night started at the Canteen, with Karla looking like she should be walking the red carpet of a movie opening. The dress she wore was blue, and her bra pushed her breasts up high and out, with men and some women wondering what they were like to play with. She danced with nearly a dozen men that night, as Peter dance with several women. At the end of the night, the dress was lying on her living room floor. The rest of her clothing was all over her bedroom as was his clothes.

What started out as another one-night stand ended on Monday morning when they both went back to work, or in her case training. Sometime during the weekend, they both determined that it was infatuation they were feeling towards each other, and Peter insisted that she explore other individuals to see if her feelings were strong enough to endure another, or shut her down because of him. Karla told him if she was free to explore, then he was also.

It took some discussion before they arrived at that conclusion, and there were no restrictions on what night during the week, but Karla stood firm in that next Friday night was once again his.

Karla pushed her physical rehab training as far as Colin would allow her to push it, wanting to get back into form knowing how much better night time activities would be once the ache in her hip was gone. Plus, the bonus of being back in a cockpit was at the end of that rainbow.

She danced nightly at the Canteen, trying to sort out which of the male species she might wish to take to her bed as she watched DeMello leave on a Tuesday night with Lucy from the hospital. On Wednesday night, she told Jennifer that the men here were all so polite and fit, that trying to determine who she might play with was difficult. Jennifer suggest Wendell Barnes, one of the computer techs from the Bunker.

Wendell left Karla's bed just after one in the morning. On Thursday night, she told Jennifer that he was a good choice, but at the end of it all, as hard as he worked to please her, she felt empty inside. Jennifer could only smile as she told Karla what she was feeling was the absence of the love that she felt with Peter. Karla started to go home alone, but changed her mind, and for the second time in her life, she slept with another female. Jennifer.

When DeMello came to her Bungalow on Friday night, she told him what she had discovered about herself, and her feelings for him. He echoed her sentiment, but they both agreed it was too soon in their relationship to say it was a firm feeling, and not one imprisoned in them because of the situation they were in.

Except for Peter being called into the Bunker for a briefing, they once again spent the weekend together, learning about each other in and out of bed.

Late Monday evening, Karla was getting ready to go over to the Canteen just to kill some time when a large aircraft landed at the Compound, then a short time later took off again. Karla was sitting with Jennifer and two others, just talking about whatever subject came across the table, when it was mentioned that Colonel Garcia and her team had just flown off to deal with whatever problem they were sent to deal with.

Karla asked why he had not said anything to her over the weekend about leaving, and she was told that missions are not discussed outside of those involved. Even people like Wendell, who helped developed the intelligence for a mission will not talk about it before, during, or after the mission outside of those directly involved. Wendell was in the Canteen and she took him to the dance floor and quickly found out he would not talk about where Peter had gone, even if she offered him another night in her bed. She left Wendell on the dance floor and went back to her Bungalow alone.

She sat in the darkness of her quarters, thinking about what she was feeling and the effects it was having on her. Could it be that this situation was one where she was looking for comfort in a mixed-up world? She was still sitting on her couch when she heard her alarm go off telling her it was time to get up.

Even though she was only working half days until cleared back to full duty, it seemed longer than normal. Once she had her gear and weapons cleaned from the days usage, she went to bed. Jennifer called her just after six to ask if she would be in the Canteen tonight. Karla went over and ate there as she just sat, and talked with the girls.

It was a comment from Maria, who worked in Intelligence that put things into perspective for Karla.

"Sexual intercourse between couples, male/female, female/female, whatever does not define who a person is. But it often defines what a person desires. Is a woman who gives herself nightly to a single man, or one that gives herself to many men all that much different from each other? I mean, except for those being paid to screw, are they truly all that different?"

No one responded, so Maria continued.

"It's built into the human genome to reproduce, and for some the drive is greater than in others, but we often mistake that drive as being overly sexed, and for a woman it is being a whore. Are we whores? Maybe. This environment is prime for a female to get laid nightly, and the men would never treat any of us like a whore found in a bar. Why? Because they recognize as many of us who have been here for a long time, that sexual contact with either sex, gives us a break from the stress of our work here."

Jennifer spoke up then.

"Look at the level of tension in the Canteen tonight. The Orchids are gone, off doing what they do, and we sit here wondering if they will be successful and all return home, or one of

77

them, maybe all of them, will return in a body bag. We're like the wives who sit at home while their husbands are deployed, wondering if our lovers will return. The only difference is we can walk across the dance floor, select a man, and for however long we wish, get some relief of that tension."

Karla sat for a long time, quietly thinking about what had been said before she asked a question of the women at her table that had been on her mind.

"I know this may be out of bounds, but when any of you first came here, did you fixate on a single male as you adjusted to the situation here?"

Maria chuckled before answering.

"I think every woman does, just like the men do with us. Karla, I do not know what your in-briefing was like, but there is only one real restriction within the Group. Married men do not serve on Operational Teams. The missions they undertake are high risk, and Colonel Garcia refuses to make a widow of a wife because of mission failure, or just bad luck. This also applies to the Valkyries. There have been several couples that have met here and married. Either they are given non-deployable assignments, or for the active duty personal, returned to their services to complete their enlistments."

"Karla," Jennifer spoke up again, "It's obvious you have a thing for Pete DeMello, and I doubt anyone here would criticize you for that. And the fact he is meeting you halfway says a lot about you. But one thing you need to know. The Orchids take the jobs with the highest risk. Those men have been with Colonel Garcia from the beginning and are so loyal to her, it seems like a cult at times. Let life take you too where ever you end up, because if you push it, you'll find yourself very disappointed."

Karla thanked everyone for their advice, then once more went home alone. As she lay in bed, she thought back to every lover she had taken. Maria was right in that sex was a great stress relief and she had used that in college and afterwards whenever she had become stressed out. Now she was tossed into an environment where it seemed odd that sex was so out in the open, but it was beginning to make sense to her.

The men and women serving within the Group knew that the teams that went out on missions may not return. Granted every time she climbed into a cockpit, there was a risk of dying, but these folks were different, more dedicated than even she had ever felt during her missions on hostile targets. And there was no doubt that Peter DeMello had a certain attraction unlike any man she had ever known. But she decided that she was not in love with him, but that the infatuation for him was not unlike other lovers she had been with. All she could do was let nature take its course and never look back.

The next four days were repeats of the previous days as she worked hard in the gym to regain her physical condition. Colin loosened up his restrictions on her exercises, but had he back in the MRI on the third day.

Her range scores were slowly climbing, and Colin was putting her through tougher courses of fire to see how she was reacting to faster times between target segments. On the fourth day he switched her up, making her change from pistol to carbine then back to pistol to see her reaction times.

She avoided the Canteen during this time as she felt it was a distraction, and spent her nights reading as she sipped on the remains of the bottle of wine that Peter had brought for dinner.

Karla had become used to the sounds of aircraft landing and taking off from the Groups airfield, and stopped wondering when one of them would bring Peter back. One landed just after midnight, which only caused her to take slight notice as it woke her up, then she rolled over and went back to sleep.

She was up and dressed for the gym when she stepped into the living room to see the door open, with Peter standing in it with his gear in his hand and looking like he had been through hell. He dropped his gear by the door, closed it, then walked up to her. She was trembling inside as he pulled her tight and kissed her.

It was nearly an hour later that they stood under the hot water of her shower, cleaning the smell of wherever he had been from his body, and the sweat of sexual combat from hers. He had a small bandage on the outside of his leg thigh that he told her was a grazing, flesh wound and not to concern herself with it.

Karla never said a word about the fact that no one knocked on her door or called to see why she was not in the gym at the proscribed time. As he dressed to go to his quarters, she dressed to finally go to the gym. Neither spoke much during their time together, just enjoyed the moment. He was careful as he leaned over to kiss her before he left so his filthy clothing did not touch hers.

As she was later walking on the treadmill, she knew what had happened between them was not two people in love, making love, but two people desiring that contact to be human again. She gave herself to Peter, so he could wipe a portion of what he had seen and done from himself. If that made her a whore, then she would play the part to the fullest, even if he never told her he loved her.

She did not see Peter again for almost a week as he left the Compound. Karla found out he had gone to see his sons. She took advantage of that time to focus on her own physical and mental health by spending extra time in the gym in the afternoon with Colin's approval and even more range time.

Before Peter returned, she was given another complete physical, then ran through the PT Test to confirm her condition. She was given a go to extend training. Karla was back to one hundred percent.

The hours training became longer, and more difficult for her as Colin pushed her hard, developing new skills and improving old ones. When Peter returned, it was not to her bed, but on the couch to talk. Both agreed their desire for each other was pure animal in nature and as much as they enjoyed being together, neither found the love that might have developed between them. Before he left her couch, he told her he would never deny her, but she needed to focus on her training, and if she took another to her bed, he would not be upset since he could never be anything more than what he already was to her. A moment in time.

It was over two weeks before she invited a man to her bed, and she realized later that Peter had been right as was the women she had talked too. It would be another month before she took another to her bed, and this time it was Peter. That night felt like the first time they had made love, but this time she understood the meaning of it all.

Her own training escalated to her entering the Funhouse on the Alpha Course, improving with each course of fire. She would transition through the courses with different partners each time to include Peter during her final course before moving to the more difficult Bravo Course.

When a 'Q' model Apache helicopter arrived at the Compound, her time was now divided between flying, and the rest of her training. This made her days even longer as now most of her Funhouse time was at night, giving her little time to spend in the Canteen, even if she went to bed alone.

One discovery that pleased her more than any was that no matter who it was, no matter their sex, she found support from everyone she came in contact with within the Group. Karla awoke to the realization she had fallen in love with those that were working hard to help her get through rough times, even if she was sleeping alone nearly every night.

A Big Decision

Karla was called to the Bunker for a meeting with Sandra and Gloria. In the conference room were also the Sergeant Major and Colin Berman. Sandra opened the meeting.

"Major Welch, according to Chief Berman and the Sergeant Major, you are progressing through your training better than expected. Especially after your injury at Benning. You're IP on the Apache has nothing but praise for your ability to fly that aircraft. According to gun camera footage, you were able to put the bird in near perfect firing positions for your gunner, and flew near perfect missions when the guns were slaved back to your position. Video of the targets you fired upon at Fort Hood, showed a higher percentage of direct hits then some experienced Apache pilots and gunners. Well done Major."

"Thank you, Ma'am. The Apache is a good aircraft, and easy to fly once you understand the nature of the craft. What's next, Ma'am"

"We are going to send you to Florida, to SOCOM, to come up to speed on several of their OPFOR aircraft. Russian, French, Italian, and such. This will include utility aircraft along with attack aircraft. According to the folks there, it should take you about six months to complete the transition."

"That sounds great General. Thank you."

"Karla, once you return, you will have a major decision to make. Step into the full-time assignment as my aide, or take a Valkyrie team as team leader."

"General, do I step into the leadership of an existing team?"

"No, the team will be built around you. We'll suggest who you accept according to standing team requirements, but the final choice is yours of who serves on the team. We'll even start team training with more personal than you need so you can trim it to your own likes. The ability for team members to mesh, to be comfortable with each other is vital, more so than talent."

"I understand General, it is a lot to consider."

"Yes, now you have two days before you leave for Florida, then the time there to consider your future with the Group. Either decision you make if agreeable with us, and without prejudice on our part. You were brought here to be my aide, and if that is what you desire, then that is what you shall be."

Karla had not slept with anyone in over a month and the night before she left, she took George Sims, one of the Razor team that she had extracted from Ecuador to her bed.

She found Florida to be exciting as she flew different aircraft during the day, but boring at night unless she was doing a night flight. Two weeks after her arrival, she allowed herself to be picked up at the Officer's Club by an Army Major. He left her disappointed but strutting like a peacock as if he had done her a favor.

It would be over a month before she allowed another man to enjoy her and the results were the same. Karla knew what the difference was between the men at the Compound and those out in regular service. The men at the Compound actually cared about the women they slept with even if only for that night, but those out in service only cared about getting another notch on their headboard.

Karla never allowed another man near her bed as she focused on flying while in Florida. Her return to the Compound was celebrated with a small party at the Canteen, then Peter in her bed later. Silently Karla wished they could find the love both needed in their lives, but she knew that would never happen. But for those few hours together, she knew that Peter was making love to her, not just screwing her for his own pleasure.

The next morning, she met with Sandra and Gloria alone in Sandra's office.

"General Grainger, I have given this a lot of thought. I discovered many differences in the personal within the Group here that I never found in service. I have eight months left on my enlistment and before Ecuador, my vision of my career was towards twenty years. The culture shock I experienced when I came here was nothing like I felt in Florida. The interaction between people here was foreign to me upon arrival, but now it is like a large family, each person caring for another. Especially a new person lost in the confusion. What I experienced in Florida was as it always was, but could not recognize because I was indoctrinated into it from the very beginning. I'm a damn good pilot as you already know, but I am not sure I have what it takes to be a Valkyrie."

No one spoke for several long moments before Sandra broke the silence.

"Karla, how do you think Gloria and I felt when Megan Conley handed us a Tiger Team and sent us out to tackle the world? I stayed on active duty for just over twenty-years, splitting my time between being a Marine Intelligence officer with MARSOC, and going into the black world of operations to remove people who were determined to ruin this world for their own pleasure. People who sought total power over others regardless at the cost of the people whom they were a danger too."

"I remember how Gloria fought the idea of leading such a team, but is now one of the best in the business. But the key to our success, to the success of the original Tiger Lily was having people around us that were not afraid to tell us no. To offer solid advice when things got confusing, then working hard to succeed. Go talk to Tomas Garcia, Gloria's father-in-law about Megan Conley's first days. Talk to Peter or any of the other Orchids about Gloria's first days. Talk to Max about my first days even though we rarely worked together on an operation, he lived with my doubts and fears."

"General, to be honest, I want to go back into the Corps and clear any misconception about myself after Ecuador. Can I do that while leading a Valkyrie team?"

"Come with me, we are going to clear up a few things right now."

Sandra stood and picked up her soft cap and headed for the door. Gloria allowed Karla to follow Sandra as she waited with her beret in her hand. They walked through the Bunker to the exit and then up the ramp. At the top of the ramp, Karla saw the Sergeant Major with a large group of men. There had to be at least forty men mingling in the parking area. The Sergeant Major called the group to attention. Sandra spoke to them.

"Gentlemen, with the success we recently had with Silk, we are considering forming another team under Major Welch, to take some load off the Orchids, and to further confuse our enemies. Major Welch is uncertain about taking a team, but I put it to you men. Who would like to volunteer to join her team, if she accepts one? If you want to volunteer, move to the left side of the ramp."

Karla was shocked that every man except the Sergeant Major moved to the left and stood quietly.

"Thank you, gentlemen, you are dismissed. The Sergeant Major has your names, and we will let you know what Major Welch decides."

Sandra turned to Karla.

"While you were gone, we decided that if you would take the job, we'd give you an actual operations team, not a Valkyrie team. The men here are independents, or team members of partial teams that have not yet picked up replacements such as the Razors. Now let's go back to my office and talk some more."

85

In Sandra's office, Karla spoke before anyone took a seat.

"General, are you telling me that you want me to take a combat team to God knows where, and go head to head with whatever target you point me at?"

"Major Welch, you have the Distinguished Flying Cross and two Air Medals for doing just that in a helicopter. Your education in engineering means you have an analytical mind and you proved in Ecuador you can think under extreme pressure. The men who make the final cut for your team will provided you with whatever knowledge and support they can as you maneuver through the training and even the execution of your missions. If Gloria and I did not think you were capable of executing such missions, we would not be having this conversation."

Gloria spoke up at that point.

"One other thing Karla, and you will understand the importance of it later. If any of those men who just volunteered to be on a team with you have been in your bed. Strike them from the roster, and never take one of your team members to bed. You'll find losing one is hard enough without having that emotional tie."

Karla understood what Gloria was saying in that she knew the story of the loss of Gloria's husband during one of her early missions. She turned to Sandra.

"How much time do I have to decide?"

"Take a week which is one hell of a lot more time than we had, than Megan Conley gave us. Take the rest of the day off, then in the morning, Colin will begin the next phase of your training, regardless of how you decide."

Karla just wandered around the compound thinking about what had been offered her. She went to the hospital cafeteria for lunch, but mostly to talk to Jennifer if she was free. Karla found she was leaning on Jennifer a lot for advice, but this time Jennifer put it back in her lap. She did agree with Gloria that she should not be sexually involved with any of the men if she took a team, even if only for a single night.

Later she was able to find time to talk to Peter. They walked the compound talking with him describing Gloria's apprehension at leading a team of men. He told her about Amita, the Silk, who had left the Group and married her chief advisor while assigned here, after they had both left the Group to return to their services.

It was when they had finally found themselves alone on one of the pistol ranges that Peter finally told her what she knew was the reality of their relationship.

"Karla, I love you, but not the way you need to be loved. I think deep down inside, you feel the same way. I'll always be near, always be ready to help you. And making love to you is a joy, but neither of us can rely on just that. Some day you will find a man who can give you what I cannot, and you'll find it easy to return that to him."

He softly kissed her.

"Thank you, Peter. I had already come to those conclusions, but hearing them from you in a way gives me a relief that I was cheating you or myself. Thank you."

"Karla, I'm going to say something that I will never admit to saying, and deny ever having said it. Gloria is a good team leader, and maybe she cares too much, but she will listen and get the job done. But she made a mistake her full, head on mission and it cost her the man she loved, still loves. If it wasn't for her son Marco, she would be impossible to work for. He keeps her grounded. Without him she would be a bitter woman who lives with that one mistake. From time to time we, the members of her team, have to gently jerk her chain to being her back to earth, but I cannot think of a better leader to follow when things get tough on a mission. If you take a team, you'll learn how tough she can be, but she will never, ever ask you for any more than she is capable of giving."

"I cannot imagine living with such a mistake. I've heard he died him her arms which had to be horrible for her. What she said about having a lover on my team makes even more sense now. But I want your honest opinion. Do I have what it takes to lead a team?"

"The advantage you have is for one, you are a Marine officer who has been trained to command under stress. You are a combat experienced pilot who has made hard decisions under stress in less time it takes to tie a shoe. The trick will be to find you good people to back you up, and get the job done. All of the men who volunteered are good men, we have to find the best for you?"

"We?"

"Karla, who do you think helped Gloria select her team? Her husband Marco. I know these men, trained with many of them as part of their training. I'll advise you as well as I can, if you wish."

"I wish. Thank you, Peter. For everything."

He kissed her once again, but this time the kiss was such, if he laid her on one of the benches, she would have relaxed and enjoyed the moment. They walked back to the main area with her telling him about the aircraft she flew in Florida. They parted company at her Bungalow with nothing more than I'll see you later.

That night, Karla watched Peter leave the Canteen with Judy from the Bunker. She looked at the men and realized she had her pick if she desired, as long as she did not pick one of the volunteers. Karla decided that she did not need a man in her bed tonight, nor a woman even though Jennifer would have been willing. She went home alone.

Karla was thankful for her decision to go home alone and get to bed early as Colin put her through what was called the Junior Obstacle course. The first two times through it was without any gear, leaving her vest and weapons in the ATV. The third time though it, she was completely outfitted and exhausted at the end of the run. But she had made it without hurting herself. Colin just smiled and told her she needed more exercise since she must not have utilized the gym in Florida.

Karla went back to the gym and pushed herself to regain that which she had lost during her time in Florida. That night she sat at her normal table at the Canteen sipping on a Long Island Tea as she made a list of the men she had slept with amongst the Group. It actually surprised her it was so short. Then she remembered with a smile that Peter had been in her bed often, even if just for the short time it took to make love.

The thought of Peter gave her an itch she considered scratching, but none of the men in the Canteen that night were ones she had already slept with, and she was not going to disable one of the volunteers who might be the perfect fit for her team if she took one for a night of sweaty pleasure.

Jennifer was sitting next to her talking to Lucy in hushed tones. Karla was thankful for the table clothes that hung low off the tables as she placed her hand high upon Jennifer's thigh and squeezed it. Jennifer moved her own hand down and moved Karla's into her crotch and just held it there as she talked to Lucy. After a minute, Jennifer turned to Karla and leaned over and whispered in her ear. Karla laughed and nodded. Thirty minutes later Karla was being driven over the edge of pleasure with Lucy down on her, and Jennifer molesting her breasts.

The next morning, Colin was standing at the Junior Course with an unknown female dressed as Karla was. She was similar in height and build as Karla, and they started the course together. The other woman finished ahead of her and was waiting at the end for Karla.

Karla was breathing hard at the end of the run and the other woman just stood looking at her. She finally spoke to Karla.

"Major, my name is Julia Berman, Colin's wife, and I gave birth to our second child four months ago. If you take a team, either an Ops team or Valkyrie, then you had better get your head out of your vagina, and focus only on getting better. You'll have time for all the sex you desire once you come up to par and get with the program."

She walked away, and Karla watched as she gave Colin a short kiss then walked over to the staging area and climbed into her ATV. Karla walked over to Colin.

"She just gave birth four months ago?"

"Yes, Major, she did." Was all he said.

"Was she a Valkyrie?"

"Yes, she was a team leader. I had an Ops Team myself. It was a hard decision to marry, but we both decided this was best for us. Karla, I can't comment on what she told you other than she knows women better than I do. How you live your life is your business, but training you and your team is mine. You are not ready for a team yet, but if you focus, you soon will be. I can only push so hard, but you must be the one that pushes the hardest. At that point my job is to ensure that you do not over do things and injure yourself."

He canceled training for the rest of the day and took her back to her quarters. As she was getting out of the ATV, he spoke again.

"Karla, you have the potential of being as good as Colonel Garcia, but you are not focused. From this point on you need to give one hundred and ten percent, twenty-four/seven, otherwise you can stop and become General Grainger's aide. Give me two months, and I'll make you something you never imagined. It'll mean ignoring parts of your body that cries out for what it wants, and parts of your body will at first cry out for what you are doing to it. But once you get to the plateau, you might find more enjoyment in the other parts. That last part comes from what Julia has told me since before we married. Tomorrow morning is the cut-off. One decision and I wash my hands of it all, with the other decision I will give you everything I have to help you achieve what I know you are capable of. The choice is yours."

Karla sat at her kitchen table cleaning her weapons thinking about what had happened to her since arriving at the Compound. She had gone from Heterosexual to Bi-Sexual enjoying the company of either sex. Last night was beyond description with two women making love to her at the same time, but it left her exhausted, and she was still feeling the effects today. Did Julia Berman know about last night? Or was she predicting the future?

As she was considering her future, she thought about her past. Karla had never failed at anything she had ever taken to task, and now it appeared she might fail because of her own inability to control her own desires.

Regardless of how or when she returned to the regular Marine Corps, her records would show she had been the Aide de Camp to a Flag Officer. Karla felt that the General would give her a modest Officer Evaluation Report which would boost her past others for promotion to Lieutenant Colonel if she stayed on active duty.

But who would she be cheating besides herself if she stepped away from what she was being offered? She went to the Bunker and located Peter, then asked him to the cafeteria where they could talk. They took a table in the far corner so not to be disturbed. She told him about what Julia Berman said, then what

Colin told her. Karla waited as Peter gave it a moment's thought before commenting.

"Honey, I'm biased here. But the main question is what do you want to do. Take a team or be an aide. Basically, Colin is forcing the decision on you. No one will think less of you if you take the aide's job. And no one outside of the Group will ever know about what you might do to protect others if you take a team. At least not until you are old and grey and write a book about it like Megan Conley did. The decision is yours to make and as I said, I'll be there to help anyway I can."

Peter was holding her hands across the table from her as he stood, raised her hands up and kissed them. He left her sitting, thinking about what she had to do. Then she thought about her flying career, and the effect it would have on other women trying out for such assignments.

In six years of flying for the Corps she had flown only three combat missions. The first two were against hard targets in support of Marine operations, but the last one had real meaning to her. How many missions had the Orchids been on during that same time frame? How many thousands, or millions of people had they protected in their silent operations which no one would ever know about.

Karla remembered her oath of enlistment and the fact she could have flown with any of the services, but she wanted her flying to make a difference. No, she had another chance to make a difference even if it was not in a cockpit.

She left the cafeteria and went to Gloria's office. The door was open, and she rapped hard twice on the door frame. Gloria looked up from what she was working on and Karla only spoke what she felt was needed.

"Colonel, I'll take a team."

Gloria looked at her for a second before replying.

"Colin said it will take two months. Are you ready for that?"

"I'll do it in six weeks Colonel, or Colin can bury me at the end of the Obstacle Course."

"We'll see Major, we'll see."

The Next Phase

Karla threw herself into her training and at night wondered if she had made a major mistake as she sat in the whirlpool soaking the aches and pains from the days training away. She no longer spent two hours a day working out in the gym, she was now spending four to five hours and drinking protein drinks to help support her body.

Her training outside the gym moved on to other aspects of leading a team with her spending hours learning about explosives and blowing all manner of things up. Here is where she got a big surprise in that Tomas Garcia was her instructor, and was quick to give her a compliment, and even quicker to give her a sharp chewing for even a minor mistake.

In the Funhouse, the Bravo Course became more and more difficult until after one hard run of seven rooms with Peter and Colin as her teammates, she was told she just completed Level Three of the Charlie Course with high marks. This was also the first time in four weeks she had anywhere near sexual contact with either sexes when Peter kissed her on the forehead, then told her to get ready for another run once the rooms were reset.

She was taking all her meals in the Hospital cafeteria where her calories were being monitored and by the end of the fifth week, her body was toned, and she was showing more definition all over her body. Karla knew she would have to buy new underwear once training was over since nothing fit right anymore except her sports bras and shorts. Even her heart shaped face was becoming more angular which she found more attractive.

Karla was running the Master Obstacle Course to include the live fire stages as she transitioned into the sixth week of training. No longer was she fighting to get out of bed in the morning to begin the next day's training, but was up and ready to go. She also found herself running with Gloria and her Orchid team doing upwards of six miles before heading to the gym and the weights waiting to punish her. The one thing she learned while running with the Orchids was that speed was not as important as consistency. Karla figured she could easily max the run on the Corps PT Test now as she could push harder over that shorter distance and still be fresh enough to tackle whatever came her way.

She was awakened by a phone call at three fifteen in the morning. All the caller said was; "live fire in thirty minutes, Range Three". Twenty-eight minutes later she was standing on the firing line of Range Three ready to take whatever target course Colin threw at her. But instead of Colin at the computer range controls, Jon Misek, also known as Orchid Four, one of Gloria's shooters was on the computer, and he never gave her a warning notice before targets began coming up. Just as the targets were fully up, the range lights went out. She dropped her night vision goggles on her helmet down over her eyes as she was drawing her pistol with her other hand.

Karla had been carrying a radio for the past two weeks and just as she completed the course of fire, the radio crackled in her ear.

"Whiskey Nine this is Range Control, leave your brass, reload your magazines and move to Range Seven immediately."

She went to an open ammunition can full of loose nine-millimeter rounds and quickly filled all her magazines and topped off the one in her pistol. She jogged to Range Seven in the dark and as she entered the firing line, she could see the targets rising on their frames. This was a combination range requiring both pistol and carbine. She never looked to see who was operating the range as she engaged the close targets first with pistol, then switched to her carbine for the distant targets. She went through three transitions between pistol and carbine before her radio crackled again as the last fired brass was still bouncing on the concrete firing line.

95

"Whiskey Nine, reload and move to the Master Course at your quickest possible speed."

Karla acknowledged the call and went to reload. She finally got a good look at her tormenter and found it was Sam Clemens, Orchids communications specialists.

When she arrived at the Master Course, Peter was standing there with a day pack in his hands. He handed it to her.

"This has three pounds of C-4 plus six caps, fuse, and six ignitors. You're wasting time, get it on and get your ass in gear, Butch."

Karla laughed as she put on the pack and cinched it snug to her body because this was the first time anyone had called her Butch in a long time.

She took the first part of the course without difficulty, then hit the real mess that was based upon the Marines Jungle Course on Saipan. As targets came up she engaged them with her carbine, then she hit her first obstacle that had not been on previous runs through this course. Karla stepped back to examine the course, then realized that was what the C-4 was for.

Karla cut a pound block of C-4 in half, rigged a blasting cap with a sixty second fuse, and ignitor. She moved on the obstruction, set the charge, pulled the ignitor, checked to see the fuse was burning, then moved back to a curve in the course and braced for the charge to go off. She was moving as debris was still falling from the blast and proceeded on through the course engaging targets as she worked her way through the water, muck and mire of the course.

She was almost near the end of the course when another obstacle blocked her path which she had to remove. Karla used the remains of the cut block to blow this obstacle. As she was moving back to the protection of the course, targets presented themselves and she engaged them as she was seeking protection from the pending explosion.

At the end of the Master Course she found Jason Horvath, the Orchids explosive expert sitting on the back of an ATV with ammunition cans, so she could replace her expended rounds. As she was reloading her magazines, he quizzed her on how she had blown the obstacles.

As she completed her reloading and explanation of the charges she set, he raised his hand and pressed send on a hand-held radio. Moments later she received another call, this time sending her to the Demolition Range. The sun was just coming up when she trotted onto the Demolition Range where she found Tomas Garcia waiting for her.

He pointed to a small, walk bridge over a span of water and told her to blow it. Karla found herself in the water, examining how the bridge was built. It was made from heavy timbers making this a hard problem for her to solve. She finally cut four charges from the remaining two pounds of C-4, rigged one side with long fuses then the other side with shorter fuses. This gave her time to ignite the long fuses, then get to the other side to ignite the short ones while still having time to get out of the water, and into a ditch fifty yards away.

She mistimed the fuses with the short ones blowing about fifteen seconds before the long ones, but when she stood up, the bridge was down in the water. Just as she turned to find Tomas her radio told her to proceed to the Funhouse.

When she entered the Funhouse, she found both Sandra and Gloria in full battle gear as she was wearing standing at the first door.

"Take the door Major!" Commanded Sandra.

Ten rooms later Karla found herself reloading her magazines once again as Sandra and Gloria walked away without speaking to her about how they felt the run though the Funhouse went. Karla was ordered back to Range Five. From there she went through the Junior Course, then back to the Funhouse where she had Peter, Misek, and Horvath as team members through ten rooms before it was done with her as the team leader.

When she exited the last room, her radio told her to stand down. Karla looked at her watch and it was twelve minutes after eleven. She was feeling the hours as she reloaded her magazines in the hallway near the exit.

Karla exited the building to find Sandra, Gloria, Tomas, Colin, and the entire Orchid crew, plus dozens of others standing there waiting for her. Sandra started clapping, then the crowd followed suit. Karla was wet, filthy, and tired, but this seemed to lift her above that feeling.

Sandra raised her hand and the applause ceased.

"Congratulations Major Welch. You passed your final exam. Tomorrow you start building your team. Go get some rest, tomorrow starts this all over again with a team in tow."

As she walked through the crowd the applause once more began, but standing beside an ATV was Peter indicating for her to take a seat. He drove her to her quarters and when he dropped her off, she asked him if he could go to the cafeteria for her, and get her a seafood salad, since she had not eaten at all today.

When he returned with the salad, she was standing in her living room nude and dripping water from her shower. Two hours later he left with her spread out on her bed, exhausted and him feeling her claw marks on his back.

Karla woke to the smell of bacon cooking and looked up at her clock to see it was almost seven, but had no idea if it was morning or night. She got out of bed and peed before looking to see who was in her kitchen. She walked into the kitchen still nude and wrapped her arms around Peter as he moved the bacon around the skillet to prevent it from burning.

"Is that breakfast or dinner?"

"It's breakfast doll, you slept through the night."

She reached down to his crotch.

"I wonder why I was so tired."

He slapped her hand.

"Enough of that. Get dressed, we have work to do as soon as you eat. Now go before I spank you with this spatula."

When she returned, he had her breakfast on the table and was seated across from her with a folder in front of him.

"Karla, this is the list of volunteers that you have to pick from. We can start now if you want."

"Let me see it first."

He handed it over to her. She looked at it as she chewed on a piece of bacon, then took a pen from her jacket pocket and struck off three names from it before handing it back over to him. He just looked at the names she marked out and never commented on why she had done that. Beside each name was their specific specialty field.

"Peter, did Gloria give you any guidance on my team?"

"She said that you could have four or five with you. I'd take five because, then you can pair off much easier."

"Sounds good. If I remember right, she said I could start out with three times the number, then trim them down till I get to my team strength."

"Well you have seven snipers on the roster, all good men with a long gun. Tom Hendricks won his spot with Gloria by outshooting others on a course set up by the Sergeant Major."

She forked some eggs in her mouth as she thought about what he had said.

"Let's do this. If the Sergeant Major is agreeable, let him set a course, then the winner gains a spot on the team. The second-place man is in reserve in case we lose the first man during training."

"That works, and I'm sure the Sergeant Major will be more than happy to set something up. Next?"

"Explosives. Do you think Tomas Garcia can arrange the same kind of testing to select that team member?"

"Tomas was thrilled to have been asked to teach, then test you. I'll talk to Gloria later about him doing that."

"Okay Peter. Medical? Any ideas there?"

"That's going to be tougher. You have two Para-Rescue, one Special Forces Medic and an Navy SEAL Corpsman on the list. All highly qualified and in good physical condition."

"Let's come back to them later. What's next Peter?"

"Communications. Here the field is narrow. All good candidates."

"That leaves me with one position left. A shooter or weapons specialists."

Karla continued eating as Peter just waited for her to comment. She washed down a mouth full of eggs with a glass of orange juice before speaking.

"I remember reading an article some years ago about a competition the Army's Rangers held every year. One of the tasks was weapon identification and usage if I remember right. Let's up it one and have those candidates go through live fires with various weapons we might come across. High man wins."

"Karla, that sounds like a plan. If I may suggest, everyone is a shooter regardless of their specialty, so why not use the same basic concept to pick your commo and medic? They've all been through the Charlie Course, but no one has gone to Level eight except you, yesterday, and the Orchids train at that level weekly. Combined high shooter from the Range Five Master Course and the Level Eight Charlie gets the slots?"

"Set it up Peter. This could get interesting."

They went over his notes to insure they were on the same sheet of music before he submitted her plans to the Sergeant Major and Gloria. He left to present her ideas with a kiss on his lips while she cleaned up the kitchen, then turned to cleaning her weapons that had been ignored while in bed with Peter.

Her filthy uniform was in the dryer and her weapons cleaned and put away when he returned with a surprise.

"Karla, pack a bag, we're going to San Antonio for four days while the tests are being set up. Gloria is giving us a ninety-six-hour pass. Move it doll, while I go get my shit together. I'll pick you up in about thirty minutes."

When he picked her up, he noticed her bag seem very light and commented on it.

"Peter dear, none of my clothes fit me like they used too, so I'm going to by some new ones, plus a couple of new bikinis. Let's go to town big man!"

101

Selection & Training

Karla and Peter returned to the Compound to find events taking shape to select her team were complete and only waiting for her to be present during the events. To keep each event as honest as possible, if an individual needed team mates to run a test event such as the Funhouse, men from other teams or married men who were qualified to run that event were being used to keep it as honest as possible. This would lengthen the testing, especially in the Funhouse, but all involved felt this was the best course of action.

Range Five could handle four shooters at a time so dividers were set between each lane to allow the shooters to only see their targets. The rotation through Range Five was done by lottery so that it would not be all medics or commo people competing against each other as an example, further isolating the competition between the candidates.

The Sergeant Major had set up a very difficult sniper challenge based upon his own abilities which no one within the Group could debate, since he was also a World Class long range competitive shooter, and had held the record for high score at the Camp Perry matches for several years before finally being bested.

Tomas Garcia insisted that the explosive expert for the team also be a shooter since his own experience on Megan Conley's Tiger Team was roughly eighty percent shooting. The combined scores from the ranges plus his testing would be the final factor in filling that position.

Captain Mattis, the Chief Medical Officer for the Group, was standing by with both a written test and a hands-on test if two or more of the medical volunteers were tied or within ten points of each other after the range and Funhouse.

Major Simone Bricker, head of Communications was also prepared to test finalists who were close in shooting scores to determine the best candidate for the job.

The stage was set for Karla to address the volunteers prior to the first shot being fired. Before she spoke to them, she had private conversations with the three men she had struck from the list. Karla explained Colonel Garcia's guidelines and that she agreed with them. In several ways her decision not to allow them to test was indeed personal since she had slept with them. Each man understood her situation and accepted her decision without complaint.

Karla stood in the back of an ATV at Range Five and addressed the candidates.

"Gentlemen, all of you are prime candidates to fill the slots on my team, but that is also the problem. Who to select and who to reject. Even without looking at your records, I know that each of you are more than capable of working with me, supporting me, and completing whatever mission command gives us."

"I want to thank you from the bottom of my heart for volunteering and give each of you a warm, good luck as you progress through the testing."

"But I give all of you this one advantage. My Marine Corps call sign is 'Butch', and each of you have the privilege of using that any place, at any time regardless how the testing turns out. I'll not waste your time explaining how I got that name, but it is funny in context."

"Now the test here on Range Five and in the Funhouse, are the same ones I had to pass before I was certified to take a team. Once my team is formed, we will shoot these same courses as often as we can to stay on top of the game, and even improve our abilities."

"Once again I wish the best of luck to each of you."

She hopped off the ATV and shook the hands of every man before leaving the range. Karla did not want to be a distraction during the testing, so she went back to her quarters to wait. At lunch, she went to the hospital and talked to Jennifer over a Chef's Salad.

"Jenn, after six weeks of being celibate, then the past four days with Peter, I think I have finally learned that sex is a great relief, but it is also a great distraction. I was not bi-sexual when I arrived here, and now I enjoy the feeling of another woman in bed with me almost as much as a man's touch. But I think it is time for me to pull back, focus on my assignment."

"Butch, if you remember, you told me the first day you were here that you were not into women. When you approached me that first time, I almost said no, but damn you are beautiful, and I just went along to enjoy you. I knew that you were stressing and there is no doubt that getting all sweaty helps relieve a lot of that stress, but I'm glad you woke up to what all of us here have discovered. Sex can be too great a distraction from what is important here. Anytime you want to talk, or even get nasty, I'll be around. But stay focused on your team."

"Thanks Jenn."

After lunch Karla went to see Gloria and they talked for over an hour, discussing the types of team training she would have to take her team through. The first phase of training would be on the Compound, developing the team work as Karla developed the additional leadership skills needed to operate on the ground with a group of people.

In this, she would learn how each man thought, how they reacted to situations, and if everything was right, bond as a tight, functioning team.

From here they would go to select locations, off the Compound, for further team training, in various environments to tighten up that bond. Gloria told her there was nothing like hanging off a cliff in the High Sierra's or in Colorado to tighten the bond between team members.

On Gloria's wall was a computer monitor which was displaying each man's scores as they progressed through Range Five. Beside each man's name was a skill indicator and regardless of specialty, the first dozen men's scores were close. It was going to be long day as they progressed through Range Five, then onto the Funhouse, where a bottle neck will occur as they could only run two teams through it at a time, staggered to prevent one team entering as another was exiting.

Gloria had formed four support teams for the Funhouse, given those individuals some time to rest before going back into the mix. Again, scores were being posted to the computer as they came available.

What Gloria never told Karla, there was already a mission for her team if they progressed through their training at a predicted rate, and the target did not advance his own agenda requiring her Orchid team to take the field.

Karla left Gloria's office and went to Supply where they also operated a barber shop and had her shoulder length hair cut to a Pixie cut in preparation for training. All she could do now was wait till the testing was complete.

Late in the afternoon, she was called to the Bunker and given an empty office in the hallway to the cafeteria. It was completely set up to include a couch for visitors. She asked for the couch to be removed and chairs placed in the room. When asked why the change, she said the door locked and the couch was soft and springy. Nothing more was said as the exchange was made.

Karla was looking at the scores on her computer monitor, noticing two red icons next to two names indicating those men had already failed to make the cut. She was working the numbers in her head when there was a rap on her doorframe. Karla looked up to see Gloria standing in her door.

"Karla, we can't use Butch as your call sign which will be the team name. So, select one."

"Colonel, since every female who has led a team has been called by a flower, and with my red hair, I think Rose is appropriate unless you have a Valkyrie team under that name."

"We do, but that can be changed to accommodate your team."

"No, leave that alone."

She sat for a minute thinking.

"How about Athena?"

"Which Athena is that Karla? The virgin or the warrior princess?" Gloria said with a smile.

"Well it's way too late to be referred to as a virgin, so it has to be the warrior." Karla smiled back at her.

Gloria laughed.

"I'll kick it up to Sandra, but I think it'll work out fine. I'm sure you are aware we leave our calling cards behind. I leave a silk, black Orchid, but I think a card with a picture of Athena in armor will work just as well."

Gloria left and an hour later, one of the maintenance men hung a sign over her door with a single word on it; 'Athena'. She had a team name now, but the team was still fighting to be built.

The range competition went into late evening as the men progressed through the ranges. By the time the last man exited the Funhouse, there were seven men who had not made the cut. Now it would come down to the specialty tests to determine who would make the team.

Karla noticed one thing about the computer roster of the candidates and that was it did not indicate what service or rank in service these men were from. Somewhere in all of that was her Number Two for the team.

It would take four days before the specialty tests were complete, and the final scores were posted. Two communications and two medics were tied in their field scores and shooting scores. The decision was dropped in Karla's lap on how to select those individuals. She sent them back to the ranges, but this time to a higher-level course of fire on Range Five.

To keep it honest, she fired that same course prior to the men giving them a benchmark to match or exceed.

During the testing, Karla only met with Peter in her office with the door always open as they discussed the scores. They both agreed they had exhausted their own desires while in San Antonio, but it was best to not tempt fate behind a closed door. Karla also avoided the Canteen during this time not because she was afraid of developing an itch that needed scratching, but because she wanted to detach herself from the others, knowing that it was rare for Gloria to go there, even for a social drink with her people.

One other thing was on her mind as the men were running their final ranges tests and that was the Team House. Each team had their own quarters under a single roof with rooms large enough for each man to have their own showers, a full-size bed, desk, and a mini-kitchen with a fold out table for eating. There was also a full kitchen in the common area, plus room for a pool table or just seating for visitors.

There were six rooms in each Team House as that was the limit on a team size. She had her Bungalow to live in but that separated her from her team, plus it added additional time on her to get up, get dressed then travel to the team house. It wasn't all that much additional time, but it was a factor in developing team cohesion.

She took the problem to Sandra and Gloria. Sandra's response took her off guard at first.

"Karla, the fact that your team will eventually see you in various stages of undressed, even nude is not a possibility, but reality. My old Tiger team watched me change from formal dress to tactical many times, and often I was nude in doing so. The same can happen to you in seeing your men is that same situation. Modesty is not a trait found in this business. Max knew about those situations and even though he accepted them, he hated the idea."

Sandra sat for a moment before continuing.

"I'm going to tell you a story that only Gloria knows. It's the reason why we do not allow any of our females to sexually interact with the target or associates. Max and I met during the California Insurrection when he was Megan Conley's Aide de Camp and I was brought into her Intelligence section. We became lovers before we moved our command into California. I took on what at first was a simple, yet dangerous mission of infiltrating the target's headquarters to plant a bug on their computer lines."

Sandra paused as she took a sip of coffee.

"What happened was I found tons of intelligence, documents strewn about the target's desk and figured on leaving with as much as I could safely carry, but the target had a different idea. I spent over two months in his bed, being his whore while at the same time I was sneaking documents out to an Operations Team covering me. When I was finally able to extract myself, due to the target fleeing the country, I was broken, ready to eat a bullet because of what I allowed him to do to me, knowing Max knew what was happening, and I was afraid the love we had for each other was destroyed. I did those things to save lives, and the use of my body saved hundreds, if not thousands, but I was broken."

Karla started to speak, but Sandra raised her hand to stop her.

"But Max would not allow me to be broken. He would not allow what I did to distract from what we had shared before I went undercover. He told me I was not cheating on him, but doing what I felt was right to take that bastard down. He married me shortly after my rescue, but the first year was hard on both of us. He was understanding, but I was still a bit broken. I will say this, watching the target die in front of me later cured a lot of my hate for myself. No, I did not kill him, but the manner of his death was long and painful after I stepped over his body after telling him who I really was."

"Karla, that is why we have that rule. In fact, I disobeyed the orders of General Conley when I did what I did. I no longer feel any hate for myself for what I did, and no longer have the nightmares of that time, but it is still a part of me. I will not tolerate any member of this command to violate that standing order. Not even the men who are working to get close to a female target. You can taunt, tempt a target with sex, but beyond maybe a kiss, that is good as it gets, otherwise I will shut you down, and bust you out of here with an officer evaluation report back to the Marines that can guarantee you'll never see another promotion."

"Karla," Gloria spoke up before Karla could. "Last year I ran an operation with the Silk as lesbian lovers. We showed a bit of affection towards each other in public, but nothing sexual in nature as we were leading the target on. The target's last sight of us was the two of us only wearing very small panties. His last sensation on this planet was of the Silk kissing him as she was pressed against his naked body and her fondling his manhood, just before I broke his neck. We may have stretched the no sexual contact to the limit there, but it would have not gone any further than that."

Karla digested what she was told, knowing that she could never repeat what Sandra had told her to anyone.

"Yes, I see the reason for that rule. And that my moving into the team house is not a problem."

Karla looked at Gloria.

"I suspect Peter has seen you nude too?"

"On several occasions. And at one time or another, I've seen all of the men nude. But that's business. Something else you have to consider is that once they move into the team house, that is also where they may bring females for the night. Be prepared for that too."

"Yes, that thought had not crossed my mind. Can I keep my Bungalow for my own use?"

"Certainly." Sandra answered.

"Thank you. Now I understand the Orchids wear Tiger Striped uniforms while the normal teams wear either Khaki or greens. Sandra, I heard that your team wore the Lizard Striped uniforms. Since your team is retired, can my team utilize that uniform?"

"Yes, but during training, they will wear Marine digitals to conceal their identity."

"That's fine. I think I have covered what I needed to ask today, although I imagine I'll have a hundred questions tomorrow. Any words of wisdom?"

Gloria spoke up.

"Go slow and build the trust between you and your team. Listen to them, but you have to make the final decisions. Trust them and your instincts."

After Karla left, Gloria addressed her thoughts to Sandra.

"From the looks of things, she is going to have a strong team. She made the right choice to allow the men to compete, which gives her the best of them. Unless something happens, I'm going to send her out to deal with Pandora."

"What's your evaluation of Pandora at this time?"

"They're stable, holding what they have. Hopefully they will stay that way until Karla is ready to get dirty. If they move before then, I'll go after them myself."

"Alright Gloria, just keep me posted."

Karla met with her team that evening after dinner in her office.

Her Number Two was Navy Lieutenant Bryan Cosby, who was also her Explosive expert. His training was in Navy UDT/EOD.

Communications was in the hands of Sergeant First Class Jack Dubois, Army Special Forces.

Medical would be dealt with by Air Force Master Sergeant Eric Cook, a Para-Rescue Medic.

Her Sniper and Number Three was Gunnery Sergeant Ron Davies. A Marine Raider.

The fifth man, her shooter and weapons expert was also a Marine. Staff Sergeant Jerome Gomez, also a Raider.

They sat in her office as she looked at their final scores.

"Gentlemen, I'm not sure if I should congratulate you, or give you my condolences, but it looks like you are stuck with me."

This drew a laugh from the men.

"We have been assigned Team House Six, and we'll move in tomorrow. Yes, you heard me right in that I will be moving into the team house also. I am aware of the rules of deportment in the houses, and if you wish to entertain one of the ladies in your apartment, then feel free to do so."

She gathered her thoughts before continuing.

"For now, we, as a team, will wear Marine digitals during training, so once this meeting is over, go see Chief Mosby and get outfitted."

"Next is our chain of command. I've written it out and it's fairly straight forward."

She handed out a paper to the men with the chain of command on it.

"There was a subject concerning the viewing of each of us with less than normal clothing discussed while in the team house. We are all adults, so let's not make big deal of the possibility. My door is always open, but please knock first. And from the looks of some of your faces, no, I will not entertain a man in the team house, and I will certainly not entertain one of the team in that same manner."

"Excuse me Major?" Lieutenant Cosby spoke up.

"Hold that thought Lieutenant. Between us, as I said before the testing started, just call me Butch. Now Bryan, what is on your mind?"

"Butch, forgive me, but this is going to take some getting used too. Not having a woman in command, but the idea of seeing that woman as nature made her."

Karla laughed.

"Gentlemen, talk to any of the Orchids. They have seen Colonel Garcia is such a way several times in training and during missions. This is something we all must get accustomed to, and we might as well start now. No, I'm not going to run around the team house in my lacey things, but the possibility of seeing me that way is a possibility. And let's be honest, none of you men have anything I have not seen before."

Again, the men laughed.

"That is all I have for now, so unless any of you have any questions, go to Supply and get outfitted. Also, if you can get lucky tonight, take advantage of the situation because we're not going to have much time for that starting tomorrow."

The men filed out to deal with Supply leaving Karla to consider what she had said about getting lucky. No, she was going home alone tonight. She cleared her computer, shut off her office lights and closed the door behind her.

Karla picked up a pasta take-out to eat at home and went to relax before the next day began. She already had her bag for the Team House packed as she sat at her table and ate her dinner. Karla was standing in her bathroom, nude and waiting for the water in her shower to heat up when she heard a noise in her bedroom. There was Peter, removing his clothes to join her.

The next morning was taken up with moving into the Team House, then going to communications to get their team radios before they hit the Funhouse for their first run through as a team. From there they went to the Master Obstacle Course and ran it as a team, then back to the Funhouse. The day ended late with the team eating together at the Bunker's cafeteria at a single table discussing how the day went.

For the next week, the days started with team physical training, then ranges followed by the obstacle courses. They were carrying day packs with rations and extra ammunition, with Cosby carrying C-4. This came in handy as the Master Course often had obstacles needing removed. By the end of the week, everyone was carrying C-4 as they also moved to the Demolition Range for training.

Two weeks into training, they suited up for a night jump and parachuted into the Sierra Madre Mountains of California for mountain training at the Marines Mountain Warfare Training Site. They spent a month in the mountains, living off the land with resupply drops every four days. The men got used to her bathing in the nude alongside them in streams, and soon no one even noticed if she was dressed, or unclothed when not in training.

They were picked up off a mountain top by a SPIE extraction system and taken to the Base Headquarters where they were bused to an airfield, rigged up for another parachute drop, then flown to Fort Irwin for three weeks of desert training against National Guard troops.

Texas was their next stop, back to the Compound where they rested for a week, then off to the swamps of Florida for two weeks. During the week of rest, she often passed one of the females from the Compound coming or going after a night of sex with one of her team members. She stayed in her apartment in the team house the entire time resting and writing up her evaluation of the training they had so far been through.

When they returned from Florida, Karla found out that Peter was off on some liaison mission for Gloria and took Wendall Barnes back to her Bungalow for a bit of relief. Her team was on stand down for two weeks, and when Peter returned, she took him to her bed for a single night, then back to her team apartment.

Even on down time she ran and exercised daily, and after a few days, her team assembled and ran with her even leaving a female on their bed from the night before.

Mozambique

Karla was lying in the brush in the Angonia Highlands of Mozambique just twenty kilometers South of the border to Zambia. They had been in the mountains for nearly a week searching for the main camp of slavers working in the area. This was the Teams first mission.

Slavery in Africa had ceased over fifty years before, but a new insurgence of this crime against humanity was once again raising its ugly head. Karla was watching through binoculars as guards moved Africans into what was not much more than large cages. She counted the guards and determined there were nineteen total, including the people who appeared to be running the camp.

Cosby, her Number Two was lying a hundred meters away doing the same thing she was doing while Ron Davies, her sniper was to her right about forty meters away ranging the targets and getting a head count.

Thirty meters behind Karla was the rest of the team, watching to insure no one stumbled onto them as they did a visual recon of the target area.

Karla ran the numbers twice before pulling back to the others with Cosby falling back with her, leaving Davies to watch the slave compound.

"What do you think Bryan?" Karla asked Cosby.

"If that long house is where they are bunking down, three claymores can deal with that. Jerome can cover the office area fairly well. But I think we are pretty much out of range for Ron to be effective."

Karla thought for a minute.

"We need to get Jack and Ron in closer. Jack can spot and keep us advise as we move in on the target. I'll be with Jerome

115

while you and Eric deal with the team house. One thing I need to do is get Jerome into a position where he can also cover that long house with his 240L. The only thing I am concerned about now is any guards that might be out and about after dark. Jack, this is where you have to keep us advised as we move on the target."

"No problem Butch. I'll stay awake just for you."

"You better or I'll take a switch to you."

They had to stifle a laugh.

"Jack, go link up with Ron, tell him the plan and have him see if there is a place further forward you two can move to after dark."

"Will do Butch."

He moved out of their position to link up with Jack. Ten minutes later her earbud crackled in her ear.

"One this is Three. I have a place spotted. Wait till I am in position and can confirm range before moving on target. Over."

"Three this is One, sounds like a plan. Advise when moving, out."

Karla checked her watch. They had two hours before it would be dark enough for Jack and Ron to move without being detected. It was nearly forty-five minutes later Ron contacted her.

"One this is Three, you need to come forward and see this, over."

Karla moved forward and when she was in position to examine the slave compound with her binoculars, she saw what Ron was talking about. The slavers had removed a female from one of the cages and were taking turns raping her on the bare ground in front of the slaves. As tempting as it was to have Ron take a shot, she just pulled back and pushed her anger deep inside.

Just at dark, everyone moved forward and waited for Ron to announce he was moving. In the faint light, Karla could see the body of the raped girl still lying in the dirt. At that distance, Karla could not tell if the girl was dead or alive.

Once it was dark over the camp, the only word from Ron was simply; 'moving'. It was nearly an hour later that he made another call; 'set'. This told Karla that Ron was in position and ready to cover their movement. She keyed her radio and gave her command to go.

It took nearly two hours before they found their final positions before moving on the camp. Jack was watching through a night vision spotting scope and advising everyone where the three guards were at. Karla moved Jerome to where he could cover the office and long house, then she moved forward to take out a guard.

Everyone was set when she stood from the brush, took two steps and put a 9mm bullet in the back of the guard's head that she was stalking from her silenced Sig P320. She moved to the right in order to remove herself as much as possible from Jerome's line of fire and waited.

She heard 'hold' over her radio, then a wet splat and a body falling to the ground before 'go' was given. She smiled as Ron had taken out a guard that must have moved out of position. In her night vision she saw Eric and Bryan move on the long house. They hung four claymores to the outside of the grass and stick long house, before moving back to a safe location.

Karla dropped to the ground as Bryan gave the warning of fire in the hole, then the long house erupted in flames as the claymores detonated via remote command with thousands of steel ball bearings ripping everything inside the long house apart.

When the first man stepped out of the office, Jerome opened fire at the targets waist ripping him apart, then sweeping back into the office. Screams could be heard from the office along with the screams from the slaves.

Karla came up on a knee, ready to engage any target that presented itself.

"Five this is One, I'm moving in."

"Roger One."

Karla moved quickly to the office, tossed two hand grenades through the open window, then flattened on the ground before they went off. She then moved to the door and entered the office, ready to engage anything moving. There were three bodies in the office, one was female, all dead.

"One this is Two, longhouse clear, over."

"Team this is One, office clear. Four check the girl that was raped. Over."

"Roger One" Four answered.

"Two, we have a lot of paperwork here. Move in and help collect it. Over"

"Roger One."

It took almost fifteen minutes picking out the papers strewn all over the office from the machine gun fire and her hand grenades. Nothing was left, regardless of how torn it was. It would be the Intelligence folk's problem to deal with it.

"One this is Four. The girl is alive, but not for long, over."

"Four, juice her, put her out of her misery, over."

"Roger One."

Karla moved from the office to the guard that was nearest the cages and found the keys to the locks on his body. This was the target Ron had taken out.

"Team this is One, everyone pull out."

As the men pulled out, they spread playing cards about the ground with the Ace of Spades on one side and the image of Athena in armor on the other.

She waited in between the cages as her team moved back towards their start point. Karla moved as far away from the cages as she felt was possible before throwing the keys at one of the cages then fading back even further into the darkness. Once she was sure one of the slaves had the keys, she turned her back and moved towards her team as Jack gave her a play by play of what was happening behind her.

A Marine Osprey picked them up just after three in the morning and flew them out to the USS Gerald Ford. From their they boarded a COD, a C-3E Greyhound for a flight to Diego Garcia to catch a C-17 for their flight home.

Karla had a nightmare as she was trying to sleep as they flew across the Pacific Ocean. She could not get that girl out of her mind as those men raped her. Bryan moved to where she was sitting and finally took her into his arms and held her as she woke, crying.

Later she pulled her team together and told them about her nightmare. No one spoke, only nodded their understanding. Karla finally was able to get to sleep without dreaming about the girl.

Karla went directly to Gloria's office when they returned to the Compound and told her about the nightmare on the plane. Gloria told her she often had nightmares after a mission, but they soon went away. Karla knew their team communications were satellite linked back to the Bunker, so they had the audio of the mission. She turned in all the body cams they were wearing, plus the cam attached to the spotting scope as part of the mission debrief.

The team was down for two weeks after the mission. Karla spent the first week in her team apartment leaving only to eat. When she finally came back to the real world, she told her team she was alright, she just had to let the nightmares run through her until they went away. She had done this before while flying when she became too stressed to deal with some things. The team knew her flying record and took what she told them as gospel.

Karla went to the Canteen that night hoping to see Peter there. She was told he was busy working on some project. She danced with several men, but as tempting as it was to drag one to her bed, she knew that would not be the answer for what was bothering her. She only wanted to talk to Peter, the one man who understood her.

She left the Canteen and went to her Bungalow, sitting in the dark, watching television. Karla was thinking about going to bed when Peter entered the Bungalow.

"They told me you were asking about me, and that you came here alone."

"Yes, I just wanted to talk. If I wanted to get laid, there were several men willing."

"Baby, I think every man in the Group including a few married men would love to get into your bed."

He walked over to the coffee table and sat down in front of her.

"I'm here Karla, talk to me."

Karla gave him a near moment by moment briefing of her first mission. Peter just sat and listened as she described the feelings she had experienced, especially when she watched that girl being raped.

She told Peter how she had to hold back from jumping too soon because of the feelings she had about the rape. But when she

120

killed the one guard she felt nothing, and tossing the grenades into the office building gave her no thrill, only the knowledge that anyone left alive in the building would be dead.

They talked for over two hours and when she was finally talked out, Peter took her by the hand and led her to bed. They did not make love as he held her as she slept. In the morning it was a different story.

Karla threw herself into exercising, even after hours to burn off her feelings. She had spent years using sex to stave off stress or feelings of depression. Karla knew she was using Peter as she had other men over the years, and even as willing as he was to make love to her, she felt guilty for using him that way. The Group was as they said, a target rich environment for a female with sexual desires, and she was determined not to get into that trap, so she avoided going to the Canteen, even to eat.

She stayed in her Bungalow the rest of the week in part, so her male team members could bring females in without guilt of running into her. Jennifer stopped by one evening with a bottle of wine, they talked as they sipped on glasses of wine, then Jennifer gave her a soft kiss before leaving without any further contact.

Karla sat in the darkness after Jennifer left hating what she had got herself into, but did not know how to escape it. It was one thing to fly above the battle even at low altitudes, but it was another thing to witness death within arm's reach even when you are the one causing that death.

In The Books

Karla walked through the lobby of the Alvear Palace Hotel in Buenos Aires as if she owned the place. She was dressed as if she was going dancing as she was wearing a thigh exposing tight, black halter dress showing a lot of cleavage, while the slit up the side of the dress showed she was not wearing any panties.

Her three-inch heels made clicking sounds across the marble floor as she moved to the exit. She exited the hotel and stepped into a waiting Mercedes with what everyone watching thought was a body guard holding the door. He closed the door for her, then got into the passenger seat as another body guard drove away.

On the seat beside her was a radio showing to be powered up. Karla picked it up, put the ear bud in her left ear, then keyed the radio to speak.

"Bunker, this is Athena Actual, mission accomplished, Over."

The delay between her calling until the reply seemed to take forever even if it was only seconds.

"Athena, this is Bunker, roger, come on home, over."

"With pleasure Bunker, Athena out."

The ride to the airport was not without delays, but they had timed it a dozen times and knew the max time it would take to go from the Palace Hotel to where they were to meet an Air Force Diplomatic Gulfstream to return them to Texas.

Jerome was driving since he spoke near perfect Spanish even if he had been raised in Idaho. Bryan was acting as her body guard. The rest of the team had been spread out covering her if needed, and they were reporting to be at the airport.

As soon as she boarded the plane and the door was closed, she took off the long, black wig and threw it in a seat, then sat down and buckled up.

Once they were in stable flight, Eric brought her a bag and moved out of her way as she stood and removed her dress, exposing her nude body to the interior of the aircraft. As she was putting on a pair of panties, Eric spoke to her.

"Butch, are you alright?"

"Sure. Why are you asking?"

"Your right breast is showing bruising, as if someone got rough with you. He didn't rape you, did he?"

"He tried but failed. Whoever finds him is going to get a rude shock. I left his cock sticking out of his mouth along with my calling card pinned to his forehead by an icepick."

No one spoke as she finished getting dressed. Once dressed, she carefully peeled off the fake fingerprints and just tossed them onto the floor of the aircraft.

They had stalked him for a week, but it was not until Karla was topless at the hotel's pool that she got his attention. She had dinner with him in the hotel's restaurant before going to his suite. His assault on her began in the elevator, and she ended it as soon as the door shut on his room with a long, stainless steel needle in his right eye socket through into his brain. The needle was concealed in the hem of the slit on her dress.

Once she had him laid out on the floor with his cock in his mouth and her card pinned to his forehead, she cleaned herself of the blood splatter on her face, breasts, and exposed skin from his eye. Her black dress would conceal such of the splatter until it was fully dry, but she dabbed the spots of blood with a damp washcloth to slow down the process.

His crime was in the trafficking of young girls for sex. It was reported that he had brutalized many of them before turning them out to service clients all over the world. Karla knew that this was just the tip of the iceberg in trafficking, but she just took out the largest player in the Southern Hemisphere.

Before she leaned back and closed her eyes, she removed the colored contact lenses that changed her green eyes to brown.

This was their fourth mission in six months, and she knew she would not have any nightmares over this one. In that time, she had not slept with either man or woman in the past two months. Once they landed in Texas, she got a message to Peter that she would be in her Bungalow and the door would be unlocked. Peter slept with Karla for the next three nights until she moved back into the Team House.

Karla lay in her bed in the Team House wondering if she could ever go back to being a regular Marine again. A year ago, she might have done what she did to the target out of anger, but there was no anger in her at any point in killing him, or doing what she did to him afterwards.

Was she becoming the Femme Fatale that she had seen in so many of the action movies her father loved to watch when she was growing up? Detached and cold blooded in her actions?

Operation Pandora

Gloria looked at Karla sitting across from her thinking she should rake her ass over the coals for appearing topless in public to attract a target. But she had been topless when she broke the neck of a corrupt Dutch politician, so that was slim difference between the two.

Then there was the manner in which she left the body. But from the reports from medical on the bruising of Karla's breast and Peter's unwilling report on her status made Gloria decide to just leave things as they were.

"Karla, I'd like for you to take thirty days leave, relax and try to get your head back on straight."

"I'm alright Colonel."

"Really?" Gloria took a deep sigh before continuing. "Karla, you took one hell of a risk going after Morales alone. He could have raped, even killed you before your support could get there to help you."

"It was a calculated risk Colonel. Sure, he bruised my breast, but we are both women, we know that it doesn't take much to bruise them. I was ready to kill him in the elevator, but most of the bruising was caused from me jerking away from him. I played along that I liked it rough to distract him and get into his suite, so I could remove him."

"And the removal of his penis?"

"That was for show. Payback for all the children he had raped. What is Intelligence discovering about that with my calling card attached?"

"Several small-time traffickers have pulled up stakes, closed up shop and moved to other locations. Local authorities have been alerted through some back channels we have access too.

For the most part, your card has frightened a whole bunch of people."

"It just dawned on me Colonel, that I have less than two months on my enlistment. Is that why you wish me to take leave?"

"No Karla, we have another operation coming up and I just want you fresh and clear thinking before I either send you out, or bench you and take it myself?"

"What's the mission?"

"No Karla. And don't think you can get it out of Wendell either."

Karla laughed.

"Colonel, no matter what I offer Wendell, or do to Wendell, he will not break the security on anything he is involved with. I even offered to let him take me in the ass once, and he told me forget it. So, you do not have to worry about him."

Gloria just shook her head as she laughed. Then she stopped laughing as she realized that it really wasn't that funny.

"Karla that worries me."

"Colonel, it once worried me, but no more. Haven't your spies told you that I'm about to become a nun? Oh sure, I played with Peter after this last trip, but it was over two months of being celibate before that."

"Fine, now will you take the leave, or do I have to order you to take leave? And I mean away from the Compound?"

"Yes Ma'am, I'll take leave. I suspect my team will also go on leave?"

"Yes, they will. Karla your team has done good work and I think they will do even more, but like you, they need to relax.'

"When to I start leave?"

"Tomorrow morning. You can drive, or we can fly you to your folks to see them if you wish."

"I take that is a hint not to go see Mike Conley then?"

Gloria smiled.

"Alright Colonel, I'll go pack and drive to see my folks."

Karla spent the night alone in her apartment then drove to see her folks outside of Seattle. It took her three days to make the drive, all the time thinking about what to do during her leave.

She arrived home on Tuesday, much to the surprise of her parents. On Saturday night, they threw a party and introduced Karla to one of Boeing's Engineers and they spent the night talking about flying. He invited her to Boeings planet to take a personal tour.

Karla dated the Engineer three times over the first week home before he made a move on her. As much enjoyment as she found making out with him, she refused further advances. They dated one more time a couple days later and once again she never allowed it to go past the kissing stage.

At the end of her second week of leave she received a registered letter. When she opened it, there was a map and instructions to go to the location on the map. The attached letter was from Michael Conley and told her to meet him there in five days. The location was called Pine Tree Lodge in Colorado. The letter said there was a room already reserved for her.

Karla figured her travel time and left with an extra day in case of car trouble or detours. She arrived a day early and decided to see if they had a room to spare until her reserved room was ready. Karla was surprised when Michael met her at the registration desk and signed her in. He then introduced her to his mother, Megan Conley. Karla had not checked the internet about this lodge, otherwise she would have seen the owners name.

Over dinner, Karla and Michael talked about her returning to Marine Aviation and becoming his Executive Officer. His command time had been extended eighteen months and he wanted her as his Exec.

When she hesitated to accept his offer, he asked if there was something holding her to the Twenty-First. He then reminded her that his Mother founded and formed the Twenty-First, and even owned the land it sat on at one time.

He asked her again if there was something holding her to the Twenty-First, and again she hesitated until she heard a familiar voice behind her.

"Butch, answer the man. Is there something holding you to the Group?"

She nearly jumped out of her chair to see Peter standing in the door of the dining room. She looked back at Michael who had a large grin on his face, then back at Peter.

"What are you doing here?"

"Answer the man Karla. What's holding you to the Twenty-First?"

"You."

"Is that all?"

"Isn't that enough?"

"No Karla, we both know that what we have is all we shall ever have. We have no real future together, only this moment in time. What else is holding you?"

"I'm afraid that I can no longer function in a regular service. I've changed too much."

"No Karla you haven't changed, but you've grown up, matured. Those are the very traits Mike needs in an Exec."

Karla looked between Peter and Michael as if confused about what to say, if what she might say would violate security. Peter spoke what she was thinking,

"Karla, Michael is one of the few outsiders that knows what the Group does. After all his Mother was its first commander. You can speak freely in front of him."

"Gloria says she has another project in line for my team. Then there is my team."

"Bryan can take over the team. You've done one hell of a job putting them together. In fact, any new teams will use your formula to build on. And as far as the project is concerned, if you really want to tackle another mission, that one should be in the books in time to give you a year as an Exec before Michael moves on. A year is all you need to take command of your own squadron."

"I have to think about this. Michael, how much time do I have?"

"My current Exec takes command of HMA-362 in three months. I can get another month before HQMC shoves an officer into the slot."

"I'll need to reenlist long before that."

She stood thinking, then looked at Peter.

"You never answered me, what are you doing here?"

"I'm here to convince you to take the Exec's job."

"Did Gloria send you?"

"No, Max did. And it was not without a fight from Sandra and Gloria. Sandra might be in command, but when Max puts his foot down, she listens. Butch, the Corps needs your talent, your example if the anti-women clique is to ever be defeated."

"So, you just came here to convince me to leave the Group?"

"Yes. Anything else is a bonus."

"When do you have to go back?"

"I can leave tomorrow, or ride back with you. Your choice."

"You son of a bitch."

"Fine, I'll leave tomorrow. Mike, you have a room for me?"

"Oh no you don't. You'll sleep in my bed because if I leave the Group, I'll probably never see you again."

"Karla dear, you will certainly leave the Group, because you know you need to before you become like the rest of us. You know that as well as I do. Now, is there anything left in the kitchen? I'm starved."

Karla spent the next day in Megan's office talking to her about the Twenty-First and her own career as the Tiger Lily. Megan told her how she tried to stay out of the business, but was drawn back into it with the assassination of President Mansfield, then the California Insurrection.

The nights were often spent in front of the large fireplace in the lodge's lobby, just snuggled up to Peter, then later snuggled up in bed even if they did not have sex.

They took two days to drive back to the Compound, spending the night is a small motel in Wichita Falls, Texas, where they made a mess of the bed.

Karla went directly to Gloria's office upon arriving at the Compound.

"Colonel, I'll take the mission you mentioned before I left, but once that is done, I'm going to take Michael Conley's offer to be his Exec."

"I know Karla, Michael called me."

"He called you? But I haven't told anyone my decision, not even Peter?"

"Michael is good at reading people and Megan is even better. Karla, I think you are making the right decision, and if you wish to stand down from the mission, I can respect that."

"No, I'll take it. But I also need to reenlist. Can that be dealt with here?"

"Certainly, Sandra is still listed as a serving officer as I am. But her being a Marine officer will make the paperwork that much more proper, even though it will say you are in SOCOM at the time of your reenlistment."

"Okay then, what's the mission?"

Gloria turned to her computer, typed in the commands and the large monitor on the wall to her left opened with the photos of a man, and three photos of a large villa, from three different positions.

"It's taken us over two years to nail this one down. We have a Russian ex-patriot, who is the head of a drug smuggling organization which we suspect is using the money from the sale of drugs, to buy and supply weapons to terrorists, insurgents in at least three different countries."

"Suspect?"

"We know about the drugs, but have yet to nail down the weapons. He's crafty. He has layers of lieutenants to protect

131

himself in those dealings. Karla, Interpol has lost two agents during their investigation of him, and the DEA has lost one. All three murdered and butchered."

Karla stood and went to the monitor to get a closer look at the photos of the villa.

"Why haven't you gone in before now to take him out?" Karla asked as she was examining the photos of the villa.

"According to solid intelligence, he has not left that villa in five years."

"Yeah, it is a bit of a fortress. My office is kind of small, so can we set up an operations center in my Bungalow, and give my team a chance to work the problem?"

"Yes, we can do that."

"Good. Set it up and we'll dig into it. Also, I'd appreciate your team in on this as advisors."

"No problem, let me get this started."

"Thanks Colonel, I'd best be getting to my Bungalow and start moving things out of the way."

As she was moving her coffee table to the spare bedroom, her team showed up to give her a hand. Gloria had called the team house, and just told them to report the Karla's Bungalow for a mission brief.

A few minutes later, two other people knocked on the door. The male introduced himself as Simon and he was their computer tech. The female was named Marcy, and she was the Intelligence tech. They looked at the front room, then put their heads together for a minute before Simon told Karla everything in the room needed to be removed except the couch. Simon then got on his phone with everyone in the room listening to him advise whoever was on the other end what he needed to set up the Bungalow.

Within thirty minutes the first truck load of cork boards and white boards arrived. Right behind them came an eighty-four-inch television modified to be a computer monitor on its own portable stand. Three eight-foot folding tables were set up which suddenly made the living room a very, small place. A computer terminal was set up on one of the tables, and hooked to the monitor, with a connection to a wall jack.

"Major Welch, how much of the paper intelligence do you wish to see?" Marcy asked Karla.

"All of it. What we determine we do not need, we can pack back up."

"Yes Ma'am." Marcy moved out of the way and made her call.

In less than fifteen minutes, two men began carrying boxes in with Marcy holding a clipboard the first man gave her, initialing off lines of the list it held, then signing off on it once the last box was in the house. There were nine boxes, the size of printer paper boxes now sitting on the tables.

"Where do you wish to start Ma'am?" Simon inquired of Karla.

"We can start with both of you calling me Karla. Let's start with the target."

As Simon put a photo of the target up on the monitor, then split the screen and placed the personal information up beside it, Marcy went into the hard copies and located the file on the target, and began tacking his photo and information sheets to the cork board.

Karla moved close to the monitor looking at the target's face. His name was Lazar Mikhail Sokolov, and he was a former Spetsnaz, meaning Russian Special Forces. Karla read his bio for anything that might help her get past the villa's gates. She tuned out the chatter in the room as she looked for a weak link she could exploit to get to him, but she figured Gloria had already done that.

"Flashing your tits won't work getting at this target." She heard Peter speak from behind her.

"No doubt, but I wonder if you in a Speedo might get his attention?" She never turned to look at Peter as she spoke.

"What, you think he's gay?"

"Not sure, but he is in his late fifties, in good health according to the last sighting, and unless there is other intelligence to correct this information, there are no women inside the compound except during the day. Then that is only a cook and house keeper."

She utilized the touch screen on the monitor and blew up one of the smaller windows.

"See, they enter around zero six hundred, then leave around eighteen hundred. Unless he is screwing one or both of them during the day, he just might be gay and is playing with the men locked inside his villa at night."

Karla looked at the information a bit longer.

"Marcy, what do we have on his physical condition? Not just his current one, but maybe something from his Spetsnaz days."

"Let me look."

"Sure, we have all day, and it was just a thought."

Karla moved everything aside and expanded one of the photos of the villa taken by drone.

"Bryan?"

"Yeah Butch?"

"Would you be a dear and contact the Bunker Cafeteria and order enough pizzas to cover this crowd since we will be having a working lunch."

Bryan chuckled.

"Sure, thing Butch. Supreme?"

"Yes, thank you."

Karla moved another photo from a different angle, then expanded it. After several minutes she closed that one then opened another.

"You looking for a way in and out?" Peter asked her.

"In is a problem, out is not." She tapped the helicopter at the rear of the villa. "That's an Airbus Dauphin Five. It has plenty of lift and space for my team to make a speedy exit. Right now, I'm more concerned about getting into that villa compound."

"Can you fly it?"

"Yeah. Now let me think"

Karla kept moving photos of the villa around examining each one with the eye of a gun ship pilot. Without looking at those around her she spoke.

"Ron, take these photos apart piece by piece. If Tom Hendricks isn't too busy helping Marcy, get his advice on a firing position. I can't find one, but maybe you can."

She looked at the specifications of the exterior of the villa, then the size of the villa itself based on the information on hand.

"Jerome, come here, and look and see if you see what I'm seeing."

Jerome moved beside her and looked at the data on the villa and its grounds. He looked at the villa from various directions before he just stood shaking his head.

"Butch, a belt fed would be useless there unless we have to hold the place from reinforcements. What are you thinking?"

"I'm thinking once we get in, we have close-quarters fighting inside that villa, with no knowledge of the layout of the rooms. According to the current information we could be facing upwards of twelve guards plus the target is Spetsnaz, so we need to make sure we go in with plenty of firepower, and then some."

Jerome looked at several more views of the villa before he responded to Karla's comments.

"P-90's. The Israeli's have developed a sub-sonic round for it that still has great penetration. Magazine capacity is fifty rounds which means we can load up with ten mags each, plus we can exchange our Sig 320's for FN's and use the same ammunition in the pistols. Silencers are no problem and can be quickly changed if we need to."

"Sounds like a plan Jerome. Go see Chief Mosby about outfitting us in that manner to include Ron. As soon as we can, we need to get on the ranges to get acquainted with those weapons."

Karla moved over to the cork board and began reading the documents Macy had posted there on the target. She was trying to absorb all the information as quickly as possible.

"Peter, I'd like your team to take that villa apart piece by piece and see if you can find me a way in. Bryan, get in on that with Peter. Jack, first make sure our communications will not be inhibited in that area, then check and double check our equipment. We can't have any glitches."

Everyone found a place to work the problem as Karla worked on the target himself. She munched on a thin sliver of pizza while moving about reading one document after another.

From time to time, she would make a comment to the white board. She had to chuckle when she saw Peter and Bryan kneeling on the floor examining the photos of the villa.

Karla ran everyone, including Peter off at seven after a catered dinner of pasta from the cafeteria. She sat in the darkened living room looking at the darkened monitor and the ghostly boards against the wall wondering how she was going to accomplish this mission.

The next morning, she asked Simon if there was any way to get a floor plan of the villa. He told her that they had searched for floor plans for months without success. She then asked if they had any infrared photos. Her gun sights on the Cheyenne could look into structures using infrared. They were not exact, but it would give them a better idea of what they had to deal with once inside the villa.

That afternoon a dozen HK P-90's were delivered along with FN pistols of the same caliber. All of the weapons and accessories had European markings instead of American Import markings. There were also twenty thousand rounds of Israeli ammunition for the weapons.

Peter and Bryan reported the only solution they could both agree on was to scale the cliff at the rear of the villa, then over the rear wall near the helicopter pad. Karla told them that was also her conclusion, but wanted another opinion.

The days were spent going over the information they had at hand, and going through the ranges becoming familiar with their new weapons.

Ron reported there was no place he could get to ahead of the others without making them wait for hours to obtain a firing position, and even then, he could most likely would not be able to cover a fourth of the target area.

The nights for Karla were spent alone, thinking about what she had to do to make the mission a success.

Simon was able to present eight infrared photos of the villa which gave the team a better idea of what the interior of the villa looked like. A second set was obtained taken later in the night, during the time frame Karla figured would be the best time to assault the villa. It only showed six, warm bodies to include two in one bed, wrapped around each other. Karla smiled as that photo was of what they considered was the master bedroom.

There was one spot in the photos that was darker than the area around it. Based on similar villa designs, that was the entrance to the wine cellar. That was an unknown they would have to deal with once inside the villa.

Karla formulated a plan to scale the cliff behind the villa, go over the wall, then leaving Ron to watch the helicopter, five of them would quietly take the villa. The ledge between the cliff and the wall was wide enough for the team to gather and wait until the last man was on the ledge before going over the wall.

She first presented it to Peter and Bryan, then to the rest of the team members including the Orchids and asked for any ideas to improve on her idea. Once everyone had their say, she made the adjustments she felt was best, then took the plan to Gloria.

That night and the next, she took Peter to her bed after night fire exercises in preparation for the mission. She woke up with Peter snuggled up tight against her by a phone call advising her the mission was a go.

The rest of the day was insuring each item on their equipment checklist for the mission was ready and packed. By dinner time, Karla and her team were flying over the East Coast towards Europe and their target.

Karla sat in her seat during the flight knowing there were still too many unknowns for this target and it scared her. She looked at her hands and they did not shake as she thought they would.

Get this one over with and see if she could make a life for herself, hopefully with Peter somewhere in it. Even if they only had moments together, she knew she would be content with her life.

Execution

Karla's team linked up with a Valkyrie team that had been in place for nearly a month. The Valkyries moved them to a point south of the villa, approximately twenty kilometers south of Vlore, Albania. The Valkyries were order out of the country as soon as the Athena team was ready to move on the villa.

It took four hours for the team to scale the cliff up to the villa. They sat on the ledge resting as they were being fed updates via satellite link on conditions inside the villa. The risk of a drone being detected and alerting the inhabitants of the villa was too high, so a CIA satellite had been tasked to provide coverage.

At two in the morning, local time, Karla went over the wall, followed by Bryan, then the rest of the team. The plan had been altered splitting the teams in to two-person groups as they moved on the villa. Karla was teamed with Jack Dubois, her Commo tech as they moved to the south doors of the villa.

Jack had sat a receiver on the wall with a retrains so the Bunker could talk to them, advise them if anything suddenly popped up which might upset or delay their plans.

When everyone was set, Karla gave the go order and she entered the villa's kitchen and killed the guard who was sitting at the table drinking a cup of coffee. Each team leaped-frogged through the house removing anyone they found as the Bunker advised them the location of a hot body in a room.

Karla met up with Bryan at the doors to the Master Suite. Jack and Ron opened the double doors with Karla and Bryan entering side by side and sprayed the bed, killing its two occupants. All rooms had been swept leaving only the wine cellar.

As Eric, her medic took the fingerprints of Sokolov to confirm his demise, Karla went to the entrance of the wine cellar. She waited until he team was behind her, then froze at the door.

She moved back from the door and keyed her radio, whispering softly into it.

"Bunker, this is Butch, confirm any movement near the compound, over."

It seemed that the response would never come.

"Butch, you are clear at this time, over."

"Roger Bunker."

Karla moved back to the door, and motioned Jerome to open it. He was crouched down as he opened the door with Karla ready to kill anyone within her line of sight. Down the steps she went with Jack holding onto her in case she slipped. The others followed and as she stepped onto the floor, she moved right as Jack moved left. Looking for targets.

In the cellar they found kilo sized packets of heroin stacked in one corner. On a table were stacks of American and European money. Karla laughed, then took her pack off and dumped out the contents onto the floor, then began to fill it with American currency.

She had everyone fill their packs and bags found in the cellar with currency, leaving nothing behind. Bryan collected the twelve pounds of Semtex-H explosives from the pile from the emptied packs and rigged them up to destroy the heroin.

Just as they were leaving, with Karla and Bryan the last out of the cellar, a hidden door opened as a wine rack swung open. Bryan was just striking the ignitors on the charges, and Karla was watching him when the first man entered the cellar, then opened fire on them as two more men entered behind him.

The firefight lasted for only seconds, but Karla was hit in the right side. Bryan had a flesh wound in his right arm during the fight. The team rushed back down into the cellar. Jerome moved to the opening and tossed two grenades down the tunnel, then swung the wine rack back into place.

"Fuse is lit, clear the cellar!" Bryan yelled.

Karla was hurting as she moved up the steps, but never commented on the fact she was hit. At the top of the steps, she called the Bunker.

"Bunker, this is Butch. We're blowing the villa. Estimate time is fifteen minutes. We're out of here. Over."

"Butch, we copy blowing the villa, over."

Karla moved as fast as she could feel the effects of her wound. It was worse than she first considered as she was feeling light headed, weak, meaning she was bleeding badly.

She made it to the helicopter and stumbled as she tried to get into the cockpit. Ron grabbed her and felt the sticky wetness of her blood on his hand.

"Butch, you're hit!"

"I know Ron, get me into the seat so I can get this bastard in the air."

Ron helped her into the pilot's seat as Bryan took the other seat, with the team climbing into the back, leaving the passenger doors locked open. She fought to focus as she powered the bird up, watching the digital gauges until she had the RPM's, oil pressure and hydraulic pressure in the green.

"Bryan, put your hands and feet on the controls and follow through with me. Do not over compensate for my movements."

As soon as they were off the ground, she turned out to sea. Somewhere out near the heel of Italy was the USS Bataan, waiting for them.

"Bunker this is Athena, I need a bearing to Rendezvous, over."

"Athena this is Rendezvous, we have you on radar. Bearing is two-one-seven degrees magnetic, over."

"Rendezvous, this is Athena, I copy two-one-seven magnetic. Have medics standing by, over?"

Karla adjusted her flight path to the bearing she was given and opened the throttle on the engines of the Dauphin.

"Athena, this is Bunker. Do you have wounded over?"

Karla was fighting to stay alert as she felt shock trying to put her to sleep.

"Bryan, see the engine cut-off switch on the panel?"

"Yeah Butch, I see it."

"When I get this beast on the deck, kill the engines and push hard on the pedals and hold them until the deck crew can chock the wheels."

"Okay Butch, how bad is it?"

She never answered him as she focused on maintaining her flight path to the Bataan.

"Athena, this is Bunker, do you have wounded over?"

"Bunker, this is Athena Three, be advised Butch is hit. Over."

"Athena Three, status of Athena Actual, over?"

"Athena this is Rendezvous, we have a visual on your running lights over."

"Rendezvous, this is Athena Two, we see your lights over."

Karla was fighting hard to stay awake as the deck lights of the Bataan came closer. Her vision was beginning to become blurry as she pushed herself to get her team safely on the flight deck.

"Rendezvous, this is Athena Medic. Stand by with Alpha Positive for transfusion. I say again, prepare for transfusion with Alpha Positive, Over."

"Medic we copy Alpha Positive, Over."

Karla slowed her approach speed as she was looking for a deck officer to bring her onto the flight deck.

"Bryan, tell me the position the deck officers wands are at based on a clock."

Bryan talked to her as she slowed her approach and fought to stay in command of the aircraft. When he told her that the deck officer was signaling down, she pushed the throttle to the bottom and told Bryan to cut the engines. The helicopter bounced once before it settled down on the deck.

Her team was out of the bird as it was still bouncing on the springs of the landing gear, and pulled her from the cockpit. Eric was stripping her vest and gear off as fast as he could, stripping her on the flight deck to get to her wound.

"Eric?" Karla's voice was weak.

"Yeah Butch?"

"Tell Peter I love him."

"Damn it Butch, stay with me and tell him yourself."

Karla never heard what he said.

After Action Report

The team sat in the conference room with each man going over the actions in the villa. Karla's plan was nearly flawless until the hidden door in the cellar. Satellite footage showed the front of the villa rising up from the explosives, then settling back down into the crater left.

The fingerprints taken by Eric confirmed that Sokolov was dead and now buried in the rubble of the villa. The final count on the money taken from the villa was over nine million dollars. Sandra Grainger told the team that each member would receive a half-million dollars from that recovered money as a bonus.

As the briefing was being conducted, Peter DeMello was sitting beside Karla's bed in the Navy Hospital in Rota, Spain. According to what he had been told, she died on the flight deck, but Eric fought and was able to bring her back.

Karla had tubes running in and out of her body replacing fluids as others were drained off her body. Peter sat there for five days until she woke up. He just held her hand as she could not talk with the tube down her throat. The first words from her lips once the tube was removed was to ask about her team. Peter told her they were safe and back in Texas.

He then told her what she had told Eric before she became unconscious. She told him she did not expect to ever see him again. Peter never told her the truth of what happened on the flight deck, only that she made it which was all that matter.

Four days later, Karla was put on an Air Force Hospital Flight and taken to Bethesda to recover from her wounds. Peter went back to Texas after two days with a promise from her she would get well as quick as nature would allow.

A week after she arrived at Bethesda, Michael Conley stopped by to tell her she had the Exec slot as soon as she could get out of the hospital.

Two months after Michael came by for his visit, Karla was released to limited duty and returned to Texas to pack her things and prepare to return to Cherry Point, North Carolina, and to assume the position of Executive Officer of HMA-467.

Peter slept with her nightly until she signed out of the Twenty-First, and drove her to North Carolina as she rested in her passenger seat. The nights when they made love it was slow and powerful for both of them knowing that soon they would part.

He stayed in North Carolina with her for her first week as the Executive Officer spending most of his time on Camp Lejeune with the Raiders.

On her first Friday, there was a Squadron Parade with the Wing Commander, and the SOCOM Commanding General present. The SOCOM Commander presented Karla with a Purple Heart for wounds suffered in a classified operation against hostile forces, and a Silver Star. The Wing Commander awarded her a second Distinguished Flying Cross for safely bringing her aircraft in while being seriously wounded during a classified operation which returned the SOCOM Operators she had picked up safely into American hands.

Karla and Peter had that weekend before he left. She told him she would wait for him until hell froze over to decide when he had enough. But she did not want him to ignore the girls back home while he was waiting. Peter told her to do what she felt was right, but things were changing at the Twenty-First, and he just might hold her to her word.

Epilogue

Karla completely recovered from her wounds and flew as often as she could, to include other aircraft in the Air Group. The Squadron did a six-month deployment to the Mediterranean, before Michael moved to the Air Group's Executive Officer job. Karla stayed as the Exec of 467 for another year before she became its commander.

Peter and Karla saw each other whenever they could with him often surprising her when he had spare time while on the East Coast. Just before she took command of the 467th, she took leave and stayed in a Bungalow at the Compound, often dancing half the night away with anyone wanting to dance, including women, before retiring to bed with Peter.

Except for Peter, Karla was celibate which she decided for herself. During her stay at the Compound while on leave, from what she was hearing, Peter was also celibate.

It was five years after Albania, and a successful three years as a Squadron Commander that Karla found herself as the Operations Officer of the Air Group. She was sitting in her office going over training reports when there was a knock on her door. When she looked up there stood Peter in Undress Blues with Silver Oak Leaf's on his collars.

"Peter are you for real?"

"Yes Karla, I am. I once told you things were changing at the Group. This is one of them. Gloria is a full bull now and I'm the Assistant Operations Officer for the Group. I've been going to college for years, before I met you to get my education up to par. This is my reward. I'm grounded Karla, and I've come to ask for your hand in marriage."

Karla was shaky as she stood up from behind her desk and walked around it to him. She pulled him inside her office and closed the door, then kissed him as if it would be the last kiss they would every share.

"Yes, I'll marry you."

Peter took a ring from his pocket and put it on her left ring finger. It was a stunning diamond.

"I know you cannot fly wearing it, but hanging with your dog tags works for me."

She kissed him again.

They married three days later in the Base Chapel. She still had two years left on her enlistment and he told her not to worry about it. They took a week's leave to Myrtle Beach with her wearing a one-piece bathing suit to hide the scars from the wound that killed her.

Peter returned to Texas leaving her with the promise they would soon see each other again. Two days later Karla had orders to the Twenty-First as their Air Liaison Officer.

Karla surprised Peter with the announcement she was pregnant on their first anniversary. She delivered a daughter in the Compounds Hospital. Three years later she gave him a son.

Karla was extended on active duty during her assignment with the Twenty-First, so she could get her twenty years in and retire. Peter continued to work in Operations, as Gloria took command of the Group and he became the Operations Officer.

When Gloria retired, Peter became Commander and put the stars of a Brigadier General on and commanded the Group for five more years before the Group was disbanded.

Two people so unalike, found each other, and grew old together.

About The Author

Leon Michaels is the author of several novels and short stories that reflect his twenty-three years of military service.   Michaels enlisted in the Marine Corps in 1970 and has memberships in the Veterans of Foreign Wars, the American Legion, the Disabled American Veterans organizations, NRA, and Rotary International.   In 1971, he married his high school sweetheart, raised three daughters and has three grandsons. He calls Creek County, Oklahoma home.